FORGED

Also by Laura Crum

FORGED

LAURA CRUM

THOMAS DUNNE BOOKS
ST. MARTIN'S MINOTAUR
NEW YORK

THOMAS DUNNE BOOKS.
An imprint of St. Martin's Press.

FORGED. Copyright © 2004 by Laura Crum. All rights reserved. Printed in the
United States of America. No part of this book may be used or reproduced in any
manner whatsoever without written permission except in the case of brief quota-
tions embodied in critical articles or reviews. For information, address St. Martin's
Press, 175 Fifth Avenue, New York, N.Y. 10010.

www.minotaurbooks.com

Library of Congress Cataloging-in-Publication Data

Crum, Laura.
    Forged / Laura Crum.—1st ed.
        p. cm.
    ISBN 0-312-32327-1
    EAN 978-0312-32327-1
    1. McCarthy, Gail (Fictitious character)—Fiction. 2. Horseshoers—Crimes
against—Fiction. 3. Women veterinarians—Fiction. 4 Santa Cruz
(Calif.)—Fiction. I. Title.
PS3553.R76F67 2004
813'.54—dc22

                                                                    2004041859

First Edition: July 2004

10 9 8 7 6 5 4 3 2 1

For Gunner and Flanigan,
two good horses

ACKNOWLEDGMENTS

With thanks and love to Andy and Zachariah, my husband and son, and all the animals and plants that share our home.

AUTHOR'S NOTE

Santa Cruz County is a real place and is much as described, but various local landmarks have been changed and rearranged to fit the purposes of the story. All the human characters are entirely imaginary; the animal characters are drawn from life. For more information about this mystery series, go to members.cruzio.com/~absnow or lauracrum.com.

FORGED

ONE

I drove up my own driveway, mad as hell. He'd better be there; I found I was saying the words out loud. "He'd better be there or this time he's had it. If that bastard pulls a no-show on me one more time, I'll kill him."

Rounding the corner at the bottom of the hill, I looked apprehensively in the direction of the barn. Damn. I heaved a sigh of relief. There it was—a white pickup truck parked in my driveway. He was here, after all.

Parking my own truck near the house, I got out and walked back down the hill toward the barn. Perhaps I would say a few kind words to the man. My horseshoer had, for once in his life, shown up when he said he would.

Being a horse vet myself, I was more than familiar with the typical client complaint: "You guys charge an arm and a leg and you always show up late." Horses were unpredictable, and it was nearly impossible to keep a strict schedule when you were dealing with a dozen or more of the beasts in a day. But even allowing for the inevitability of delays, Dominic Castillo was notoriously unreliable.

1

There were plenty of horseshoers on the central coast of California, some of whom were quite dependable. I put up with Dominic for one reason: He was a master farrier and my horse, Gunner, had a tricky foot problem. Thus I dealt with Dominic's legendary tardiness and absenteeism.

Dominic had failed to show up for the appointment I'd scheduled last week; naturally, he had an excuse. Swallowing the angry tirade I longed to deliver, I'd rescheduled for today. As I approached his pickup truck, I schooled my face into a quiet, composed mold—not friendly, not hostile. Dominic had one more annoying fault—he was an incorrigible flirt.

No matter how often I declined his offers, advances, and invitations, if I so much as gave him a warm smile, Dominic was certain to come on to me once again. None of this was particularly flattering; Dominic was known to come on to any woman he met who was roughly between the ages of twenty and sixty. It seemed of no matter to him that he'd gone through two wives and numerous girlfriends already. Nor did he seem to care if the objects of his various flirtations were married or otherwise involved themselves. Any woman who would respond to his charm was fair game, apparently—at least in his estimation.

And he had considerable charm. Despite everything, Dominic Castillo was difficult to dislike and easy to smile at, and there you were—with the man's arm draped around your shoulders and his eyes smiling into yours as he asked you out yet again. Thus I composed my face to remain in a neutral frame.

Gunner was tied to an oak tree in the spot where Dominic usually shod him, and looked at me inquiringly. I walked up to my horse and rubbed his forehead. Gunner, my big bay gelding with his white blaze, high socks, one blue eye, and friendly nature, had been my buddy for many years now. I was more than willing to pay the top dollar that Dominic charged in order to keep my good horse sound.

Shoeing tools lay on the ground, the forge was chugging away in the back of Dominic's pickup, but I could see no sign of the man anywhere, which was odd.

I looked around the barnyard, fearing yet another contretemps. Would I find him sitting in the barn drinking whiskey? I was, after all, his last appointment of the day, and Dominic was known to like a drink. My friend, rancher Glen Bennett, always said that Dominic could shoe a horse when he was drunk better than most men could sober, but my preference was not for a drunken horseshoer.

"So, where is he?" I asked Gunner.

The horse pushed his muzzle into my face and I blew gently into his nostrils—a typical horse-greeting mannerism. Gunner's breath smelled warm and sweet, and I rubbed the underside of his neck, where he liked to be scratched.

"Dominic," I called out.

No reply. Now this was truly odd. Usually if Dominic did show up, he worked. Yes, he would flirt and chat, but he still got the job done. So, what in hell was going on?

Maybe he *was* drinking in the barn.

"Dominic," I said again, looking in the direction of my hay barn.

It wasn't much of a building—a small, high-roofed pole barn suitable for storing a load of hay; that was all. There was a good-sized stack of wheat hay filling it now, delivered a week ago by my local feed merchant. Walking towards the stack, I called Dominic's name again.

Still no answer. But I stopped dead.

Something not right. Boots . . . boots sticking out from behind the haystack. I took a cautious step forward and peered around the high wall of hay bales.

"Oh . . . my . . . God." I could hear my own voice; it didn't sound like me, though.

Dominic lay faceup in the litter of chaff on the floor of the barn. There was a bloody, wet spot in the middle of his stomach, pulpy and dark. His eyes were closed.

"Dominic!" I stepped toward him and reached for his wrist.

His eyes stayed closed, but the pulse was there, barely. Even as I took it I was digging my cell phone out of my pocket.

"Oh my God," I said again, my gaze riveted to Dominic's body as I dialed 911.

"I need an ambulance right away. A man's been shot; he's still alive," I said without preamble, knowing that the operator would have my address already.

"Is the injury serious?" the voice on the line asked.

"Very. He's gut-shot."

"And you are?"

"Dr. Gail McCarthy. I found him here in my barn."

"An ambulance and police will be right there."

"Thanks," I said. As I ended the call, Dominic's eyelids flickered.

"Dominic," I said, reaching for his hand.

The eyelids lifted. Dominic's brown eyes looked straight at me.

"Gail." I could barely make out the whisper.

"I'm here," I said. "I'm with you, Dominic. The ambulance is coming." I squeezed his hand gently. "What happened?"

A long, long silence. Dominic's lids dropped back down; I thought he was out again. But in a minute the eyelids slowly lifted and once again I looked into Dominic's eyes. I couldn't fathom their expression.

His lips twitched. Faintly, very faintly, the words came. "I was cleaning the gun. An accident." Then his eyes closed.

I pressed his hand to comfort him, hardly believing what I had just heard. Why would he be cleaning his gun in my barn in the first place?

Scanning the littered straw around us quickly, I saw it. Sure enough. Half-buried under his thigh; I'd never noticed it in my haste to get help. A pistol, looked like a large caliber. My God.

"Dominic," I said again.

No response. I thought his breathing sounded more labored. In the distance came the thin wail of sirens.

4

I sighed with relief. "Just hang in there, Dominic."

The minute or so that it took the ambulance to pull in seemed like an hour. Dominic grew perceptibly paler as we waited. But eventually the flashing lights were in my driveway, and I was waving the paramedics toward the barn. A dark green sheriff's sedan was right behind them.

Once Dominic was on a stretcher and in the ambulance, I turned to the man who had gotten out of the green car. Strongly built, with a big chest and a thick neck, he had wiry brown hair, brown eyes, and a somehow familiar face.

"Are you Gail McCarthy?" he asked.

"I am." Something in his tone or his stance made me bristle. "Dr. Gail McCarthy. And you are?"

"Detective Johnson of the Santa Cruz County Sheriff's Department." He didn't offer a handshake; neither did I. "You dialed nine-one-one and reported that you found this man in your barn."

"That's right."

"He was already shot when you found him?"

"That's right."

We were both silent as Detective Johnson made a note. I was pondering my reaction to the man, which was one of instant dislike. Why, I wasn't quite sure. A certain sort of forceful overconfidence in his voice, maybe, a tinge of that typical cop's distaste for a member of the general public. Whatever it was, Detective Johnson's manner antagonized me. I wasn't about to volunteer anything. Let him ask.

"Do you know this man?"

"I do. Dominic Castillo. My horseshoer."

"Do you know why he was here?"

"Presumably to shoe my horse." I gestured to Gunner, still tied to his tree.

"Tell me how you found Mr. Castillo."

I recounted my movements as accurately as I could, ending my story by pointing at the gun, which was still lying in the straw on the barn floor.

Detective Johnson made notes as I spoke. At one point he looked up. "He said he shot himself?"

"That's right."

"Are you sure?"

"I'm sure." I shut my mouth firmly on any comments I might have made. Detective Johnson didn't need my opinion.

I watched as the man took a cell phone out of his shirt pocket. "Could you please wait here?" he asked.

Leaving me stranded in my own driveway, he walked far enough away that I couldn't hear him, and began talking on the phone.

Since I could see no reason not to, I moved the few steps to where Gunner stood tied and began to rub his neck. In five minutes or so Detective Johnson was back.

"Please wait where you were asked to do so. This is a crime scene."

"I'd like to put the horse back in his corral and feed him and the others."

"That will have to wait until we're done here."

"And when will that be?"

"I don't know."

I could feel the annoyance building up inside me. "I expect to be able to feed my horses," I said sharply. "Do you know Detective Jeri Ward?"

"I do." Something in Detective Johnson's voice said, And what of it?

"She's a friend of mine," I amended lamely, already knowing it would do no good.

Detective Johnson visibly shrugged; I thought I saw a brief flash of outright hostility in his eyes.

I tried again. "How long will this horse need to stay tied here?"

"Until the crime scene investigators are done."

"And how long will that be? Give me an estimate."

Detective Johnson met my eyes. "I just called them. I imagine it will take them at least a couple of hours to go over the scene."

"So you don't think this was an accident?" I asked.

Detective Johnson didn't reply to the question. Instead, he asked me another. "How well do you know Dominic Castillo?"

I pondered a minute. "Not well. But I've known him, or known of him, in the way one knows a horseshoer, for several years."

"For how many years has he been your horseshoer?"

"A little over a year. But I knew him before he was shoeing my horses. I'm a horse vet; he's a shoer. We both interacted in the same community of horse owners. I saw him from time to time; I knew his reputation. I can't really remember when we first met."

"You say you knew his reputation. Explain."

I started to open my mouth and stopped. What should I say here? More important, what shouldn't I say? There was a lot that could be said about Dominic, but did I want to be the one to say it?

"He has a reputation as an excellent craftsman" was what I did come up with.

Detective Johnson looked at me sharply. My hesitation wasn't lost on him.

"And personally?" he asked.

"I don't know him personally," I hedged.

Our eyes met. At that moment a white van pulled into my driveway; both of us glanced in that direction.

"Crime scene investigation team," he said briefly. "Could you wait here, please?" And off he went to confer.

I stayed where I was told, this time. No point in aggravating the man further. He seemed to have taken the same instant dislike to me that I had taken to him. I stood quietly in my driveway and watched the crime scene team deploy themselves over my barnyard.

There were at least half a dozen of them, all dressed in beige jumpsuits, two holding cameras. They photographed Gunner; they photographed Dominic's shoeing tools lying on the ground; they photographed his truck, the barn, and, repeatedly, the gun. Others went over the ground closely, searching for something, it seemed. Detective Johnson spoke to one or another from time to time. Occasionally he made calls on his cell phone.

I waited. Time passed. The sun dropped behind the ridge and the golden slant of late afternoon light dissolved into the cool colorlessness of dusk. Gunner nickered at me from his tree. At the sound, my two other horses, Plumber and Danny, neighed loudly in unison. "Feed us," they said.

Staring impatiently at Detective Johnson's back, I tried to bore holes in his head with my eyes. *Come on, you asshole, get on with it*, I thought but didn't say.

Apparently unaware of my mental daggers, Detective Johnson continued his conversation for a solid ten more minutes before he turned to me.

By this time, I'd had it. Pretending patience for over an hour had worn me out. Wisely or unwisely, I greeted Detective Johnson's approach with a curt "I need to feed my horses and get on with my evening chores. Let's see if we can arrange that."

"You can put the horse in his pen and feed him now," he said. "But I want to talk to you a little more. Can we go somewhere quiet?" This last with a pointed look up my driveway.

"All right," I said resignedly. "Just let me get all my animals fed and we'll go on up to the house."

TWO

The last thing I wanted was to invite Detective Johnson into my home. However, common sense dictated for once. After all, it was starting to get dark outside. And I clearly wasn't going to be done with this guy until he was ready.

Ushering him in the door, I waited, almost automatically, for the positive response most people gave to my house. Detective Johnson didn't smile; he didn't gaze in appreciation. He merely glanced around briefly and sat down at the table.

Chagrined despite myself, I sat down, too. I liked my house to be admired. Its design wasn't my doing, but I delighted in its compact 650 square feet of living space, and thought my main room, which did duty as living room, dining room, office, and kitchen, to be a particularly pleasant place.

Big windows overlooked my garden, rough pine planks lined the walls, a primitive wool rug from Turkey decorated the mahogany hardwood floor. With the last daylight filtering through the high clerestory window, the room seemed soothing and welcoming to me.

Not for long. Detective Johnson was opening his notebook and looked pointedly at the light above the table. I turned it on.

"I take it you don't believe this was an accident," I said.

"We need to investigate all possibilities," he answered smoothly.

"But why would Dominic lie to me?" I asked, more or less to myself.

Detective Johnson gave me a noncommittal look and said nothing. I could fill in the blank perfectly. If he said anything to you, was what the man was thinking.

For the first time it dawned on me that Detective Johnson probably considered me a suspect in Dominic's shooting, and that I hadn't helped my position any by repeating Dominic's words, improbable as they sounded.

"I had a hard time believing him myself," I said. "Why in the world would he decide to start cleaning his gun in my barn in the middle of a shoeing job? He hadn't finished, you know. The horse only had three shoes on."

Detective Johnson gave me a quick look and made a note. Judging by his expression, he hadn't noticed.

"How well do you know Dominic Castillo?" he asked.

"I told you that," I said. "Not well. He's my horseshoer. I've known him awhile."

"Are you friends?"

"No."

"Have you ever been involved with each other?"

"Involved? Oh, you mean as in dating him. No."

Detective Johnson watched me closely. "No?"

"No," I said firmly. "Why do you ask?"

"I made a few phone calls," he said. "Dominic Castillo is reported to be a man who is flirtatious with his female clients."

"That's true," I said.

"Is he flirtatious with you?"

"No more or less than with anyone else, I imagine."

"But he is flirtatious with you?"

"Yes," I said, exasperated. "Of course he is. He flirts with everyone."

"Is Dominic Castillo married?"

"Not that I know of. Last I heard, he was living with a lady named Barbara King."

"Do you know Barbara King?"

"Yes," I said. I sighed. At this rate I would be here all night answering questions about Dominic's personal life, which, unfortunately, I did know a good deal about. Perhaps the laconic approach was a mistake.

"Look," I said, "how about I tell you all I know about Dominic Castillo, and then you leave so I can make dinner."

Detective Johnson met my eyes. "I may need to question you further."

"Some other day," I said. "Tomorrow even. Not tonight. Deal?"

Detective Johnson sat up straighter in his chair. "As long as you agree to further questioning, I'll be happy to limit tonight's session," he said formally.

"Okay. Here goes. I think Dominic's been married twice, though I couldn't swear to that. His first wife, that I know of, is Lee Castillo, and she has two kids by him. Lee has horses. She's a client of ours."

"How old is Dominic Castillo?" Detective Johnson interjected.

"Somewhere between forty and fifty, I'd guess. He's . . ." I paused and for the first time in this conversation, smiled. "He's well preserved, you could say."

Detective Johnson didn't smile back. "Which means?"

I shrugged. "He's a handsome man, if you like that type. Tall, slim, olive-skinned, dark eyes, unwrinkled, very manly and charming. Hard to tell his age, if you take my meaning."

Detective Johnson made a note and said nothing.

"Anyway, his second wife is Carla Castillo," I went on. "I know her because she has horses, too. No kids there, I don't think. For the last couple of years Dominic has lived with a lady named Barbara King, who also has horses and is a client of mine. And, as your informant told you, he's a big flirt; I certainly wouldn't know about his other conquests, but by all accounts, he had them.

"Now," I stood up, "I'm happy to give you more information tomorrow or whenever, but I'm tired and hungry and I need to make dinner now."

Slowly Detective Johnson stood up as well. "The crime scene team will need to finish up down at the barn," he said.

"Fine. So long as they don't let the horses out of their pens."

"I'll be by tomorrow."

"Fine," I said again. All I wanted was to get the man out of here. "I'll expect you."

Detective Johnson gave me yet another hard-edged cop stare and turned at last to go. No good-bye, no thank you forthcoming. I watched his departing back with relief.

The minute he was out the door, I turned to my cupboard and got out tequila, orange liqueur, and some lemons. In another thirty seconds, more or less, I had a much-needed cocktail in my hand and was letting my yapping Queensland heeler dog out of her pen.

"I'm sorry, Roey," I told her. "No running around tonight. Too much going on. Come on in the house."

I could see lights, vehicles, moving human figures down at the barn. Resolutely I turned my face away and ignored them. Nothing I could do about it now.

I dialed my lover's cell phone.

"Hello." Blue's voice.

"Hi. Where are you?"

"At work still. We're shorthanded."

"Oh." I knew how it was. Blue was the nursery manager for a large rose growing operation. Like horses, the needs of plants varied dramatically and were not always amenable to human plans; Blue was often late getting home, as was I.

"You'll never guess what happened. I found the horseshoer in the barn, shot."

A long silence. Then Blue's voice, sounding hopeful. "April fool?"

"What? Oh. No. It is April Fools' Day, isn't it? But no, no joke."

"My God. Is he all right? What happened?"

"I don't know if he's all right. He was alive when the ambulance took him away, but he didn't look too good. And I've got cops all over the place. It's kind of a weird story; I think I'm a suspect."

"What?" Blue sounded truly alarmed now.

"Don't worry; they haven't arrested me yet. But come home as soon as you can, okay?"

"Right. Will do." And we hung up.

I leaned back in my corner of the couch and sighed. Took a sip of my drink and patted the dog, who had settled herself next to me. Did my best not to look out the windows in the direction of the barnyard. What a lousy ending to what had been a relatively easy Friday.

Until now. Now it was a particularly difficult Friday. I took another long swallow of margarita, straight up. For the first time, I let my mind drift back to Dominic's face when he'd spoken to me. I wrinkled my nose. He'd smiled. I could have sworn he smiled.

But why? It had clearly cost him tremendous effort to speak. How could he have managed to smile? And again, why?

I sipped more margarita and tried to will my mind away from Dominic. Tried, once again, to take in my peaceful, much-loved room. I stared at the graceful curves of the moss green armchair in front of the woodstove. Blue's chair. Blue would be home soon.

My live-in lover. I smiled. In theory, Blue lived in his travel trailer, parked just beyond the vegetable garden. In practice, he lived with me.

Which was just fine. Blue and I had been living together a little over a year now, and I was quite happy with the arrangement. We each pursued our own lives, our own careers, and we came home to each other. I had never known it could be this good.

Sipping my drink, I sighed again. The last thing in the world I wanted interrupting my life was a police investigation in my backyard. But that was exactly what I had.

I picked up the phone and dialed a number from memory. Detective Jeri Ward had given me her cell phone number last fall. I just hoped she hadn't changed it in the interim.

"Ward here." She answered on the second ring.

"Jeri, it's Gail, Gail McCarthy."

"Gail. Oh-ho." Something in her voice, something I couldn't place. Amusement, cynicism, sympathy?

"Have you heard?"

"Dominic, the horseshoer, was shot in your barn. Matt Johnson is investigating. Lucky you."

"Lucky me," I agreed. "I think Matt Johnson suspects I shot Dominic. He seems familiar, Matt Johnson. Should I know him?"

"He investigated Nicole Devereaux's murder, a couple of years ago."

"Oh." Now I remembered. I'd met Detective Johnson briefly when a friend of mine had been killed. I hadn't liked him much then, I recalled.

"He's no friend of yours; is that right?" I asked Jeri.

"That's right," she answered crisply. "Can't say more right now."

"Have you heard anything about Dominic?"

"He's dead, poor bastard. Died in the ambulance on the way to the hospital."

"Oh no." I felt as if someone had punched me in the gut. Somehow I had never believed that Dominic would actually die. "Oh no," I said again.

14

"I'm afraid so." Jeri's voice was level—she knew Dominic; he shod her horse, too.

"That's terrible. Have you heard the story?"

"Parts of it. Look," Jeri said. "I can't talk now. Call me when I'm at home this weekend."

"Okay," I said. "Thanks, Jeri."

I hung up the phone, staring straight ahead blindly. Dominic was dead. It changed everything. I had just assumed that he would live, spend time in the hospital, recover. Without really thinking about it, I'd believed that I came in time to save him.

But I hadn't. Dominic had died anyway. After saying those improbable words. Once again, I visualized his face. No mistake. I still thought he'd been trying to smile.

I shuddered. Smiling when he was about to die. Why? Why?

Finishing my margarita in one swallow, I got up and walked across the room to the kitchen. I opened the sleek stainless steel refrigerator and evaluated. Then I opened the freezer. Frozen lasagna it was.

I turned on the matching stainless steel oven and plunked the lasagna in. Headlights coming up the drive caught my eye. Familiar headlights.

I reached down the terra-cotta tile counter for the cocktail shaker. Blue was home.

THREE

How are you doing?" were the first words out of Blue's mouth.

I met his eyes across the room. "All right. But Dominic died. Do you want a drink?"

"I guess so. Gail, are you all right?"

"I'll have another," I said, pouring myself a second round.

Blue took a step toward me and accepted the cocktail glass from my outstretched hand. "Gail, are you all right?" he asked again. The little spotted dog at his heels wagged her tail.

"I'm fine. Frozen lasagna okay for dinner?"

"Sure." Blue stared at me with obvious worry. "Can you sit down and tell me about it?"

"Okay," I said. Seating myself on the couch, in my usual corner, I watched Blue take his accustomed seat in the armchair. Freckles lay down next to his feet. Only a year or so of living together and we already had these routines, just like an old married couple.

"Well," I began, "I came home from work . . ." and told the story all over again.

Blue listened with few interruptions, as was his way. When I was done, he said, "How do you feel?"

I took a deep breath. "Knocked sideways, I guess. Like I just got kicked in the stomach. It's not really grief. I wasn't that close to or fond of Dominic. But, my God." Words failed me.

Blue left his chair and came and sat next to me on the couch. Putting his arm around my shoulders, he drew me close to him. "It must have been a pretty big shock," he murmured.

"It was," I said into his shoulder.

Freckles jumped up on the couch next to Roey, who snapped peevishly at her.

"Now girls," Blue admonished them.

Both dogs flattened their ears submissively, looking for all the world like a couple of sisters who had just been chastised for squabbling. Freckles lowered her white, whiskery muzzle down on her front paws and wagged the tip of her feathery tail. Roey licked my hand.

"Okay," I said. "Good dogs."

With Blue's long, solid body pressed against my left side and the two dogs curled up against my right, I felt sandwiched in warmth. Taking another sip of my drink, I twitched my shoulders and leaned back, feeling some of the tension ebb out of my body.

"Its not just Dominic," I said, "though that's bad enough. I feel invaded. All those strangers down there, tramping all over my barnyard. Hell, they wouldn't even let me feed the horses until they gave the word." To my surprise, there was a catch in my voice.

Blue squeezed my shoulders gently. "I understand," he said.

"And there's bound to be an endless amount of questioning; that detective is coming back tomorrow. He's an ass," I added, more or less to myself.

"Why do you say that?" Blue asked.

I shrugged. "It's hard to put in words. He's one of these men who have a sort of aggressively macho posture. I never get along with that sort. I think I push all their buttons. They seem to find a confident, forthright woman who is neither interested in them as a man nor particularly intimidated by their masculinity, a threatening commodity."

"I never knew you were a closet man-hater." Blue grinned at me.

"I am not," I said indignantly. "I just don't like assholes, whether they're male or female. Or, for that matter, black, brown, or white."

"A reasonable point of view." Blue finished his drink in one swallow.

I held up my glass. "I'll have another."

"All right."

Getting to his feet, Blue crossed the room to the kitchen counter and began making another round. I stared. Tall, long-legged, with a broad back and wide shoulders—my lover looked good from behind. Red hair curled down just over the collar of his blue denim shirt; suddenly I wanted to dash across the room and put my arms around his waist.

"Do you really think this detective suspects you of murdering Dominic?" Blue asked over his shoulder.

"I can't tell. He's got so much of that reflexive cop mannerism, you know, never-trust-a-member-of-the-goddamn-public. But he might. After all, it does sound pretty weird. Me telling him that Dominic said it was all an accident."

"Are you sure that's what he said?"

"Positive. And I could swear he smiled."

"That is weird."

"On top of which," I went on, "I still have to finish getting the horse shod. He's only got three shoes."

"A minor problem," Blue said, handing me a drink.

"Not so minor. Farriers as great as Dominic are few and far between. And if that hind shoe isn't exactly right, Gunner will go lame again."

"Who will you use?" Blue asked.

I took a sip of my third margarita. "Tommie Harper, I guess. She's the best I can think of."

"A woman?" Blue sounded surprised.

"That's right. There are women horseshoers, you know."

"Takes someone with a strong back."

"True enough. And Tommie Harper has got one." I took another sip. I was starting to feel better now. "Funny thing. Tommie lives with Dominic's ex."

"As roommates?"

"Roommates and lovers," I said.

"Oh."

"Yeah. Carla left Dominic for a woman. I don't think he ever got over it. He hated Tommie with a passion, which is something Detective Johnson would no doubt be interested in."

"Will you tell him?"

I shrugged. "I don't know. I won't lie, if he asks me directly. But I don't want to bad-mouth anyone."

"Dominic was something of a womanizer, wasn't he?"

"Oh yeah. He was your true womanizing horseshoer—it's a relatively common breed. As far as I can tell, that's how he met all his wives and girlfriends. He came out to shoe their horses, came on to them, and there you are."

"From what I heard," Blue said, "he got himself in a lot of trouble. Some of his conquests were married to other people."

"Uh-huh. There was a rumor recently that he was messing around with Tracy Lawrence, and that Sam Lawrence had threatened to kill him. Oh." I set my drink down so abruptly that some margarita splashed onto the end table. Mopping it up with my shirttail, I met Blue's eyes. "What have I said?" I murmured.

"Something that your friend the detective would be quite interested in, I imagine."

"The trouble is, it's just too easy to think of people who might have wanted to murder Dominic."

"Maybe somebody went ahead and did it."

"Then why would Dominic say it was an accident?"

"Protecting the person, perhaps."

"Protecting his killer? Why?"

"Hard to say."

I sipped more margarita. "I can't imagine why he would do that."

Blue shook his head; red-gold curls brushed his collar and sprang back.

At the gesture, I got up and walked around behind his chair. Twining my arms around his neck, I bent down and kissed his cheek. "What do you say we forget all this for a while and retire to the bedroom?"

Blue reached an arm up and gently pulled me forward so our lips were almost touching. "Margaritas make you amorous," he murmured. "What about all those people down in the barnyard; the bedroom doesn't have any curtains."

"We can turn out the lights. They can't see in." I kissed him again, on the mouth this time.

Blue smiled. "What about the lasagna?"

"It won't be ready for a while." Our lips connected for a good long while. "Don't you want to go to bed?" I asked when we broke apart.

"What do you think?" Blue asked, and guided my hand to his belt buckle.

I smiled. "Then let's go."

FOUR

Saturday morning dawned bright and clear. Venus floated in a turquoise-blue sky above the eastern ridge as I peered out the bedroom window. All the vehicles and people seemed to have vanished from my barnyard overnight.

Pouring myself an early cup of coffee, I left Blue to sleep and wandered outside to investigate, Roey and Freckles at my heels. A sweatshirt was enough to cut the morning chill; spring had definitely arrived. The wisteria vine that twined from one pillar of the porch to the next was dripping with blossoms, their dusty lavender hue a pale gray in the dawn. Early roses were in bloom, too; the banksia that covered my garden shed was spangled with frothy, pale yellow stars—a color that glowed even in this dim light. And the last of the glorious deep blue ceanothus bushes were in full cry, though their cobalt shade, so brilliant in sunlight, was ashen without it.

I tromped down the hill to the barn, coffee cup in hand, pursuing one of my favorite occupations—looking at the garden. I was finding that I enjoyed observing the plants more than anything else. Noticing their individual peculiarities, seeing how they changed from season to season, how they competed or failed to compete with the other plants. Mine was a wild garden, where introduced exotics mingled freely with the native plants, and animals, of the California brush. I had found that for every pretty piece of flora I put in that thrived, there were at least a dozen casualties. And I was also finding that it really didn't matter.

I liked to watch what happened, see what the garden itself wanted to do. Gardening was a dialogue with Nature: How about this, I'd suggest, with a clump of vivid mandarin orange crocosmia. No chance was the reply; gophers like them. Well, maybe this graceful cream-colored tea rose. Nope. Not vigorous enough and a particular favorite of the deer. Sometimes the answer was yes. The last of the brilliant yellow daffodils bloomed in long grass at the feet of blue-flowered ceanothus and rosemary shrubs—a fortuitous combination that Nature had agreed to wholeheartedly.

The garden was fun. I could feel my spirits lifting as I strolled down the border that lined my drive and noted that the mintbush from Australia was just coming into full bloom. Now that was a really spectacular plant—a solid mass of bright lavender flowers.

I rounded the corner of the driveway that led to the barnyard and my high spirits took a sudden dive. Yellow crime scene tape was everywhere, reminding me only too forcefully of yesterday's fiasco. It looked as though the cops had confiscated Dominic's truck; it was gone, anyway.

Feeding my three horses, I duly noted that all seemed lively and healthy and Gunner wasn't bothered by his missing shoe. Still, I knew well enough that I'd have to take care of it soon or risk having him go lame again.

The flock of banty chickens clamored to be fed, so I threw some hen scratch out for them, and was reminded by a plaintive *meow* that the barn cats were waiting, too. I smiled.

My old cat, Bonner, had died last winter, of complications caused by old age. Within a month of his passing, a gray feral cat had taken up residence in my barnyard. In another month it was apparent that a gray feral mama cat and her three teenage kittens were now living in my barn. I'd eventually trapped all the cats, given them their shots, and had them spayed and neutered respectively. None of them were really tame, but they did show up to be fed, and they kept the barn free of mice.

I greeted them by name as I scooped some cat food out of a barrel and poured it in their bowl. "Hi, Mama Cat," to the matriarch—not exactly a creative choice. The biggest kitten, shorthaired and jet black, was Jiji, named after the black cat in *Kiki's Delivery Service*, one of my favorite animated movies. The tabby was Baxter, for the cowboy poet Baxter Black, and the smallest kitten, black and fluffy, with white paws and a white chest, was Woodrow. This last for Woodrow Call in Larry McMurtry's *Lonesome Dove*.

I stood for a moment, watching my cat family eat while the chickens pecked vigorously at the hen scratch and the horses munched their hay. Roey and Freckles trotted through the long, dewy grass. It was all so peaceful and serene. And there, in the barn, marked off with yellow tape, was the place where Dominic Castillo had fallen, shot in the stomach.

Sitting down abruptly on a bale of hay, I stared at the spot. There, exactly there, was where Dominic had been lying when I found him. I tried to imagine him taking a break from his shoeing job to clean his pistol. Had he carried a loaded pistol with him? Jesus. I certainly hadn't known that. Why would he choose to clean it with one shoe left to tack on my horse? With his forge burning? Why not clean the gun when he was done, if he chose to do it at all?

None of it made any sense. I could definitely see why Detective Johnson might suspect me. Dominic's words sounded false, even though I had actually heard them.

Why would he lie? To protect someone, Blue had said. If the person had shot him, though, why protect them? It seemed ludicrous.

I gave up thinking, finished my coffee, and started back up the hill to the house. It wasn't my business to solve this case, I reminded myself. Right now, my business was making breakfast. Pancakes, I decided. It was the weekend, and I wasn't on call. Pancakes for breakfast it was.

We were halfway through them when I spotted the dark green sheriff's car pulling up the driveway.

"Oh no," I said.

Blue glanced at the clock. "Eight on a Saturday morning. Our detective gets to work bright and early."

The car didn't even hesitate at the barnyard, just pulled right up to the house. Detective Johnson got out of it.

"Well, now you get to meet the man," I told Blue. "Let's see what you make of him."

In another moment Detective Johnson was standing next to the table, not seeming the least abashed at having interrupted our breakfast.

I introduced him to Blue. The two men shook hands, Blue rising to do so. I was amused at the contrast. At six and a half feet, Blue towered over Detective Johnson, who was not a short man. This didn't seem to sit well with the detective, who tipped his head back to meet Blue's eyes with a scowl. With his thick neck, heavy shoulders, and square-jawed face, Detective Johnson reminded me of a bulldog; he had short, wide, thick-fingered hands to match. Blue, on the other hand, though tall and wide-shouldered, had slender fine-boned hands and a refined look about his cheekbones and eyes. A Thoroughbred, I decided. And Detective Johnson was one of those old-fashioned squatty-bodied Quarter Horses you didn't see so much of anymore. They even called them "bulldog"-type horses.

Suddenly I noticed that both men were staring at me. Detective

Johnson had apparently asked me a question; I'd been so engaged in drawing human/horse parallels I hadn't even noticed. You've been working too hard, Gail, I told myself.

"I'm sorry, I didn't catch what you said," I said out loud.

Detective Johnson wanted me to recount yesterday's story again, in detail. He wanted to know the exact time I had driven in my gate, the exact time the shoeing appointment was scheduled for, the time I had dialed 911. Some of this I could tell him; some I couldn't.

"The appointment was for four o'clock. I drove in close to five; I looked at the clock in the truck on my way home; it was four forty-five, and I remember thinking how early I was getting home. I have no idea when I called nine-one-one. I don't wear a watch and probably wouldn't have noticed the time if I did."

"Does twelve minutes after five sound about right?"

"I guess so," I said, and looked at him sharply. "You knew." And then, "Of course, the nine-one-one operator."

"That's right. What did you do between five o'clock and five-twelve?"

"I told you," I said in exasperation.

"Tell me again. Take it one step at a time. You parked your truck where?"

And so it went. On and on. Half an hour later I protested that I had told him Dominic's exact words yesterday and the detective gave me a level look in return. "This is potentially a felony homicide investigation; I'm sure you want to help us in any way you can."

"That's right," I said wearily.

"Then let's go over it again. I have all the time in the world."

I shut my mouth firmly on the "I don't" that sprang to mind. Blue leaned back in his chair in the corner and watched us, saying nothing. I noticed that Detective Johnson's quasi-hostile manner had abated somewhat in Blue's presence. Apparently I was more palatable as one half of a couple than I had been as a lone woman.

It took a long, long time. The clock said ten-fifteen before Detective Johnson seemed satisfied that I'd recounted my movements and observations exactly. But he wasn't done yet.

"What can you tell me about Dominic Castillo?" he asked.

"I told you what I knew yesterday," I said. I was sulling up, as horsemen say. I'd had enough of this grilling.

"Do you know anyone who might have had a reason to kill Dominic Castillo?"

I took a deep breath. "Dominic was a real lady killer, to use an unfortunate term," I said, "as I think we discussed yesterday. Obviously he made a lot of people angry. There was a great deal of gossip about him in the horse community. As our veterinary clinic is the primary horse clinic in this county, I know a lot of the people in the local horse community. So I heard plenty of rumors about Dominic over the years. However, I am not going to name off all the people who might have had a grudge against Dominic as a list of potential killers. There's too many, for one thing. And I'd certainly forget about some candidates and remember other rumors that are entirely false. So I'm not going to pass on any gossip. If you come up with some evidence linking a person to this crime, if it is a crime, and ask me about that person specifically, I'll do my best to tell you what I know. Now," I said formally, "I think it's time for you to go."

I met his stare. Detective Johnson's eyes were dark brown, and plainly angry. I was aware of Blue's quiet, observing gaze from his place in the corner.

"I may need to question you further." Detective Johnson rose from the table as he spoke.

I said nothing. After a minute, the detective turned without a word and walked out the door.

"I can see why you don't like him," Blue said.

"What was I supposed to tell him," I demanded. "That the current rumor is that Sam Lawrence threatened to kill Dominic over Tracy?"

"No, I see what you mean," Blue said. "Who's Sam Lawrence?"

"A horse trainer. Has a place up on Summit Road. Mostly breaks and trains backyard horses. Sam's a redhead, like you. Has a temper, unlike you. And Tracy is young, blond, and cute. You do see what I mean?"

"Yeah."

"And, of course, I have no idea if it's true. Horse people love to gossip. Tracy might not have had anything to do with Dominic. Who knows?"

"I see what you mean," Blue said again. "Kind of rough to sic the detective on them."

"That's what I thought."

"So what now?" Blue asked.

"How about we forget all this and take the horses for a ride on the beach?"

"I've got an even better idea. It's supposed to be warm and sunny all weekend. How about we take a mini–pack trip? Just an overnighter. I know a great place we could go. It's right on the beach," I suggested.

"How will we feed the horses?"

"Just leave it to me. Give me a couple of hours to get everything ready. All you have to do is get in the truck when it's time to go."

"What about Gunner's missing shoe?"

"It's a short ride and all on soft ground. We'll put an EZ Boot on him."

"All right," I said. "I'll clean up the house, weed the veggie garden, make us a lunch, and be ready to leave around one."

"You've got a deal," Blue said.

FIVE

I climbed into the truck at one-fifteen. As promised, Blue had organized everything; dogs, horses, and gear were all loaded in the truck and trailer when I walked down to the barnyard carrying saddlebags packed with a lunch on one side and a jacket and clean underwear and socks on the other. It was a relief to turn my back on the crime scene tape and drive away.

"What are we going to eat for dinner?" I asked Blue.

"Don't worry, I took care of it."

"And breakfast?"

"Took care of that, too."

"Great," I said, and concentrated on watching the landscape slip by outside the windows.

Rolling hills were vivid with the sharp chartreuse green of spring grass, splashed with yellow-orange California poppies and pools of deep blue wild lupine. Even the live oaks, so stately and somber, were warmed with the gold and rose tints of their buds and new leaves. Life burst from every twig.

The truck topped a rise and I could see the blue curve of the Monterey Bay ahead of us, looking impossibly clear and dreamlike on this sunny April day. Blue followed Highway 1 down the coastline, giving us glimpses of scrub-covered dunes, sandy beaches, and twisted cypress trees. When he turned onto a familiar side road, I looked at him accusingly.

"You're taking us out to your work?"

Blue pulled the rig into the driveway of Brewer's Rose Farm without a blink. "We're starting here, yes."

He drove through the maze of warehouses and greenhouses and parked the truck and trailer out back, next to a new greenhouse range.

"This is where you used to live, isn't it?" I asked.

"That's right. My house trailer sat just where that greenhouse is sitting now. When I kept my horses out here, I took lots of rides down on the beach. I thought I'd take you on my favorite little trip."

"Okay."

Brewer's Rose Farm was less than a mile from the ocean. We could see the deep turquoise-blue of the water and hear the distant rumble of the surf as we saddled the horses and ate our lunch on the tailgate of the pickup. When we were done, Blue adjusted the pack rig on Plumber's back and I slipped the plastic EZ Boot over Gunner's barefoot right hind. Then we pulled the cinches tight and climbed aboard.

Gunner grunted slightly as he felt my weight in the saddle. Danny stiffened as Blue settled himself; I saw the colt's head go down and his back hump up.

"Look out," I said.

Blue just smiled. Clucking to Danny, he urged the young horse forward. Danny took two stiff-legged steps, as if he were walking on tiptoe, dropped his head another notch, and launched into a buck. Blue sat on top of him as peacefully as if the horse were strolling rather than crow-hopping.

It didn't last long. Blue let Danny buck for half a dozen hops, while the dogs ran around him, yapping with excitement, then tugged on the reins and said, "That's enough." When Danny didn't respond, Blue used the end of the reins to spank the colt lightly, which brought his head up right away. Blue walked him in a circle for a moment and then untied the packhorse and rode off. The dogs and I followed.

"My goodness," I said as we trooped down a dirt road between fields of artichokes and strawberries, headed towards the bay. "Why do you think he did that?"

Blue shrugged. "He's young; he feels good; I haven't ridden him in a week; he's a little bit cinchy. All of those things. It's not a big deal. He's fine now."

It was true. The bay colt walked along as quietly as if he were twenty-five instead of five, his acrobatics temporarily forgotten.

"Better you than me," I said. "I just don't have the experience to cope with that. I'm sure glad you do."

Blue just smiled.

I remembered how easy Danny had been to train when I'd purchased him a year and a half ago as an unbroken three-year-old. Blue had helped me with him every step of the way and had taken over as trainer at my request when I felt that I'd gone as far with the colt as I was capable of going. Danny had begun bucking when he was fresh— something that I was entirely unequal to.

"Why does he do that?" I asked Blue again. "He never used to."

"It's not uncommon," Blue said. "He's just starting to wake up, feel his oats. Sort of like an eighteen-year-old kid who's always been docile and obedient and suddenly gets himself arrested for drunk driving. The parents are aghast, but it's more or less a normal stage. Danny's just being rebellious."

I looked at my bright-eyed bay horse and was deeply grateful for Blue's long years of experience breaking and training horses. Without Blue, I might have felt like giving up on Danny, seen his bucking as incurably "bad." At the very least, I would have been afraid to ride him, which was bad enough in itself.

Instead, I sat comfortably on my old and trusted buddy, Gunner, while Blue quite happily took the kinks out of Danny. What a deal.

Warmed up now, the three horses plodded quietly down the road, the dogs trailing in their wake. I could smell the briny, seaweed smell of the ocean mixing with the earthy scent of freshly turned agricultural fields. Seagulls screeched; my heart sang.

We passed an abandoned farmhouse, faded and weathered to a silver gray. Some rusting tractors crumbled silently in the sagging shed alongside. The road rose up into the dunes.

Up one hill and down the other side. Up again and there it was—a great, shining, restless bulk—the ocean. Sleek and aquamarine far out, heaving translucent green in the nearby breakers, frothy white at the shoreline. Gunner snorted.

Then we were moving out onto the sand of the beach while the dogs ran ahead to frisk in the waves. The tide was out and the wet sand along the water's edge was dark and smooth, shiny and firm. We made our way in that direction, the horses sinking deeply into the dry sand with every stride.

All three geldings had been ridden on the beach before; still they approached the surf with trepidation—eyes wide, plenty of long, rolling snorts. Gunner jumped as a little wave rolled towards us and I clutched the saddle horn tightly. Gunner had always been a spook, and even now, at a mature ten years, he still had that tendency to leap sideways. Since he was in every other way an entirely calm and reliable horse, I forgave him his one fault and cultivated a good grip on the saddle horn.

I glanced over at Blue and saw that Danny was marching along calmly, which was also typical. Bucking aberrations aside, Danny was an amazingly quiet, easygoing young horse. Plumber trooped in his wake, patiently carrying the loaded pack bags—again, a gesture that was indicative of this willing, kind, and always helpful horse.

31

So we rode, our dogs beside us; it came to me that we were the perfect family. I felt a sudden joy in the moment, all of us together at the beach, just so. Dogs running through the waves, horses moving reliably and happily along; this was the life I wanted.

I looked over at my partner, aware that he was an integral part of this picture. Blue sat peacefully on Danny with a slight smile that I thought reflected the same content I was feeling. The ocean breeze ruffled the red curls that stuck out from under his gray fedora; his long, slender, slightly freckled hands held Danny's reins and Plumber's leadrope with a touch that was both firm and relaxed.

I knew that touch; I'd experienced it myself many times. Blue met my eyes and I smiled.

"This is fun," I said.

Blue smiled back. "We live in paradise," he said simply.

I followed his eyes as they took in the long, blue sweep of the bay, the empty white sand of the beach, the soaring, screeching gulls and churning waves.

"It's true," I said. "People come from all over the world to vacation in a place like this and we live here. I sometimes forget how lucky I am; I get wrapped up in my work and feel so busy and frantic I don't even notice how beautiful this area is. And then we come here and," I waved my hand at the scene, "I realize it all over again. Thanks for bringing me."

"My pleasure," Blue said.

"And it's low tide, too. That's lucky. It's so much easier for the horses to walk on the firm sand."

Blue smiled. "I checked my tide chart."

"You thought of everything, didn't you?"

"I tried." Blue smiled again.

"Look," I pointed. A sleek humped back with a dorsal fin rose out of the surf in a curling leap.

"There's another one." As Blue gestured, I saw the shadow shape again, outlined in the shining wall of a breaker.

"Porpoises, right?"

"Yeah," Blue said with a grin. "They're surfing. Watch."

Sure enough, the animals were riding the breaking waves, exactly like human body surfers. Periodically, they would leap entirely out of the water in exuberant, frisky arches, apparently playing.

We watched, entranced. The horses marched on, unaware or uninterested in the dolphins surfing beside them. The dogs trotted behind us, tongues hanging out, tired of chasing the shorebirds.

"Hey," I said, "there's a seal."

The round, whiskery head bobbed up not far from the porpoises.

"Look at the gulls." Blue pointed. "There must be a school of fish just offshore."

Seagulls swooped low over the stretch of water where we had seen the seal; in another moment a dozen brown pelicans flew into view, aiming for the same spot. As we watched, each pelican flapped steadily into position, hovered a split second, and then plunged head-first with a splash into the water, disappearing completely beneath the surface. When they emerged, the seagulls dive-bombed them, trying to steal fish out of the pelican's beaks.

"Wow," I said.

"It's amazing, isn't it?"

Blue and I stared at the teeming stretch of seawater, awash with darting, swooping bird and animal life.

Beyond the turbulent blue-green bay the distant hills rose behind the town of Monterey. Gunner's black-tipped red ears flicked back and forth in front of me as he walked; I reached down and smoothed a long strand of his mane back in place. Then I smiled at Blue.

"We live in paradise," I repeated quietly.

33

We rode in silence for a while. Eventually Blue indicated the flat sheen of standing water ahead of us.

"Elkhorn Slough," he said. "We go inland here."

Reining Danny to the left, he led our little troop back through the soft sand and up and over the dunes. Once again I found myself on a dirt road rolling through fields of artichokes and strawberries. The roar of the ocean receded behind me. To my right I caught glimpses of a large body of quiet water reflecting the long slant of late afternoon light.

"So," I asked Blue, "where are we going?"

"Not too far," he said.

"Good," I said. I was getting tired. No two ways about it, I was out of shape. A three-hour ride wore me out. Too many long days at work; too few hours in the saddle.

The dogs were tired, too. They padded along, tongues hanging low, no more racing about. Gunner's neck was wet with sweat.

The road ran endlessly between hilly cropland, or so it seemed. Eventually, I saw a tree-filled rift ahead of us. Blue guided Danny to a narrow trail that led down into the trees.

A minute later and I gasped.

"We're here," Blue said.

SIX

The old barn in front of me was about as picturesque a thing as could be imagined. Hidden from the road by its screen of trees, it was weathered and gray and appropriately frayed on the edges, but still standing sturdy, straight, and well-shingled. The large central doorway was wide open, as was the matching opening on the far side. Through the window thus created, I could see the glow of sunlight on water. The barn looked right out on Elkhorn Slough.

"This is great," I said to Blue as I climbed somewhat stiffly down from Gunner.

"Just wait," he said.

We tied the horses to the hitching rail out front. Blue put a hand under my elbow and led me inside.

The interior of the barn was dim and cool. A huge, old-fashioned wooden hayrack and manger ran along one wall, looking in good repair. A couple of bales of clean alfalfa hay sat in the corner nearby. The dirt floor was tidy and neat, no piles of boards or rusting equipment anywhere to be seen.

Gentle pressure from Blue's hand led me on, through the doorway on the far side of the barn.

"Oh," I gasped.

It was magical. The barn sat right on the bank of the slough; some thoughtful person had built a deck along its length, looking out over the clear, reed-fringed water. A small wooden pier extended out to an island about thirty feet offshore. Sparks of light clung to the ripples lapping the planks; a long-legged blue heron fished in the shallow water just off the island.

I looked at Blue. "This is wonderful."

"Do you like it?"

"Yes," I said. "The understatement of the century. How did you find it?"

"The guy who owns this place farms next door to the rose farm. He told me about it. His family uses it once a year for a big family picnic. He said I was welcome to come here."

"And the hay?"

"I brought it one day last week when I had some time. Thought it would come in handy if you wanted to take a little pack trip with me."

"And here we are." I smiled. "You really did think of everything."

"Maybe," he said. "Ready for a drink?"

"Sure. Let's get the horses unpacked."

Blue ran water from a rusty spigot to rinse and fill an old watering trough next to the hitching rack while I unsaddled and brushed Gunner and Danny. Then he unpacked Plumber as I watered the other two and tied them to the manger with flakes of hay in front of them. When Plumber was similarly provided for and the dogs had had both a drink and a dip in the trough, we began unpacking the gear.

"Wow, it's the deluxe trip." I grinned.

Blue had brought folding chairs and a cooler. He'd also brought big, comfortable quilted flannel sleeping bags and a thick air mattress to sleep on.

"No tent, though," he said. "I figured we'd sleep on the deck. If it rains, we can just move into the barn."

"You bet," I said. I was investigating the contents of the pack bags and finding that Blue had provided us with chips and salsa as well as margarita makings. And the cooler contained a bag of ice cubes, marinated skirt steak, and a green salad.

"Wow," I said again.

"Sit down and relax." Blue indicated a chair he had set up in a patch of sunshine on the deck. "Let me bring you a drink."

"This is just too good for words." I accepted a clear tumbler filled with lime green liquid. Staring out over the quiet water of the lagoon, I asked, "What did I do to deserve it?"

"Oh, just being you is plenty, Stormy." Blue clinked his glass against mine.

"To us," I said.

We drank.

After a minute, Blue began collecting driftwood, margarita in hand. Piling it next to a simple stone firepit near the shore, he pointed at the little island at the end of the pier. "Hummingbird Island. Do you want a tour?"

"I sure do."

"Better leave the dogs behind."

We tethered Roey and Freckles to the posts of the porch and I followed Blue down the narrow, creaky pier.

"The rancher told me about this island," Blue said. "It's really fascinating."

The pier ended at a sandy spit of a beach, fortified at one end with piled rocks, which seemed to form a rudimentary seawall. The island itself looked to be less than an acre, mostly covered with native scrub—greasewood, ceanothus, manzanita.

"Come on." Blue took my hand. "Let me show you where the hermit lived."

"Hermit?"

"Yeah. Bob, that's my rancher friend, said that when he was a boy, an old man lived out on this island. A crazy old man, or that's how everyone thought of him. He had no particular right to be here; the island belonged to Bob's family, who own this ranch. But Bob's father let him stay."

As Blue talked, he led me down a narrow trail, really more of a tunnel through the brush; we both had to stoop and push branches out of our way. The path emerged into a clearing; with a wall of scrub on all sides, it was as private as if it were an enclosed villa.

"There's what's left of his hut." Blue gestured at what appeared to be no more than a pile of sticks; adjacent to it, and still standing, was a primitive arbor made of found wood. A wild cucumber vine still trailed over the trellis, wreathing it in bright green leaves and tiny cream-colored flowers.

"What's that?" I asked, pointing at a large hump in the center of the clearing.

Blue shrugged. "Sculpture? Religious icon?"

The hump was made of earth that looked as though it had been patted and stomped to a smooth clay texture. Embedded in it were thousands of shells, and fragments of shells, and pebbles, mosaic-like, arranged in strange, swirling patterns. At the top, an intricate geometric shape radiated outward.

As I stared, a tiny, iridescent green bullet dive-bombed my head, with a sharp, whirring shriek.

"Yikes." I ducked, already recognizing the culprit. "Hummingbird Island," I said to Blue with a smile.

"That's right. They're all over the place. They breed and nest out here."

"That one looks like an Anna's," I said. I was familiar with hummingbirds; they nested on my property, too.

"I think so," Blue said. "From what I've seen, there are both Anna's and Allen's Hummingbirds on this island."

I looked around the clearing in bemusement. "So this old man just lived out here alone with the hummingbirds, making weird sculpture?"

"That's right. When he first came, apparently he had a little boat, which he used to row to the town of Moss Landing for supplies. After he got older, Bob's family built the pier, so they could bring him food."

I smiled. "Their own personal hermit."

"Yeah. They probably got lots of karma points for taking care of him."

I stared around some more. The clearing had an eerie resonance; it felt entirely apart from the modern world. I could almost sense the old man's presence, brooding over his strange mound. Not hostile, not frightening, just otherworldly.

Blue watched my face. "Can you feel it?"

"Yeah."

"That's what I thought, too. It's an odd spot."

I raised my eyebrows. "A sacred space?"

"Maybe." Blue sketched a small, formal bow in the direction of the mound. "We'll be going now."

"Thank you," I said, nodding my head in the same direction.

We both ducked back into the brush, emerging onto the sand spit by the pier. Startled, a mallard female herded her flock of fluffy babies back into the water with many alarmed quacks. Blue and I stood silently together, hand in hand, as the ducks sailed off in a tiny flotilla.

"That was neat," I said as we walked back along the pier. "Thank you for taking me there."

"My pleasure." Blue grinned. "How about another drink?"

"You're on."

We drank margaritas while Blue made a fire and grilled the meat; he'd brought red wine to drink with the steak and salad for dinner. The sun went down over the lagoon as we ate; afterward Blue emerged from the barn carrying two oil lamps.

"I stashed these here when I brought the hay," he said, as he lit and hung the lamps off the deck. "Watch. There's something I want to show you."

The lanterns cast a flickering illumination over the slough. As it grew darker, I found that by cocking my head so I got the angle just right, I could see into the inky water.

Blue smiled and pointed with his eyes. "Hold still," he said.

A flap of wings alerted me to a black bird with a white crest descending out of the night sky to perch on one of the posts that formed the porch railing. Two others arrived right behind him.

"Night fishing herons," Blue whispered softly.

This was a type of bird I'd never seen before. As I watched, the three birds studied the water below them intently. Suddenly one plunged, as neatly and precisely as a high diver; he entered the water headfirst and appeared to swim under the surface briefly. His head popped up a second later, a silvery fish in his beak.

I smiled at Blue and reached for his hand. Together we watched the birds fish for what seemed like a long time; it might have been only ten minutes. I was lost in the magic of the scene, the old barn at our backs, the slough before us, the fitful light of the lanterns on the water. The diving herons, with their long, trailing white crests, like plumes, lent just the right note of exotic splendor.

"This has been the perfect vacation," I whispered in Blue's ear.

He smiled and reached in his pocket. Before I could see what he was doing, my hand was in his hand.

"Stormy, will you marry me?"

"Will I what?" I looked down in amazement. Blue was gently

pressing a ring into my palm. My fingers closed around it and I held it up as I met Blue's eyes.

"I'm sorry," I said, as I saw his expression. "I wasn't expecting this."

I looked at the ring. A simple band, it was set with a heart-shaped stone that flashed in the dim light. It didn't appear to be a diamond.

"It's a sapphire," Blue said. "It was my mother's. I had it set in a ring for you."

I swallowed.

"Sapphires were always my favorite stone." Blue looked down.

I took his hand. "I don't know what to say. Thank you for asking me. I honestly hadn't been thinking about us getting married."

"Will you think about it?"

"Of course. Tell me, why do you want to get married? Don't you like things the way they are?"

Blue gave me a hesitant glance. "I thought," he said diffidently, "if we wanted to have a child, it might be better if we were married."

"A child?" Now I was really reeling. "You want to have a child?"

"Haven't you thought about it?"

I was silent for a moment. "Yes," I admitted, "I have."

"Me, too," Blue said simply.

"Is that what you want, then?" I asked him.

"Maybe. If you do. Either way, I'd like to marry you. I love you, you know."

I smiled. "I love you, too. No matter what."

"So you'll think about it?"

"Yes. I promise."

"Good. I'll save the ring until you decide." Blue pulled me towards him and gave me a long kiss.

"Maybe," I said, when we broke apart, "we should just skip straight to the honeymoon."

"Those sleeping bags look awfully good," he agreed.

I kissed him one more time and began to unbutton my shirt.

Blue grinned. "I can't wait to see what you look like by lamp-light," he said.

SEVEN

I arrived home the following afternoon to a reality check of truly dismal proportions. Crime scene tape still swathed my barnyard, Detective Johnson had left three messages on my answering machine, and Gunner was lame. Despite the EZ Boot and the soft ground, the trip had really been too much for him.

"Damn." I watched my good horse limp off across his corral and wanted to kick myself. "I should have got the shoe back on him right away."

"Why don't you call the shoer now while I feed," Blue suggested.

"All right." I headed back up to the house, mentally composing what I would say to Tommie Harper. It wasn't exactly a typical request. Please finish the shoeing job your competition started. And Tommie was a very forthright person. I'd just have to see what she made of it.

Tommie laughed. "So Dominic managed to get shot in the middle of shoeing your horse?"

"Is that what people are saying?"

"That's what I heard."

"Well," I said feebly. "Would you mind putting the last shoe on? It's the foot the horse has got navicular in, actually, and he's already sore."

"No problem."

"I've been using an egg bar shoe with a wedge pad," I added.

"No problem," she said again. "I'll be there tomorrow evening when I'm done with my appointments. Say, five-thirty."

"Great," I said. "I appreciate it."

I hung up the phone noting that Tommie had quite distinctly failed to say that she was sorry about Dominic. Of course, it was no secret that she'd detested the man.

On the thought, I dialed another number.

"Hello." Jeri Ward's crisp tone was unmistakable.

"Jeri, it's Gail McCarthy. Are you busy?"

"No. I'm home, I'm off duty, I'm not even on call. How are you doing?"

"Fine, more or less. I was just wondering what the story was on Dominic."

"It's a strange one. And your part is the strangest. Old Dominic's last words."

"I know," I said. "But that's what he said. I heard him."

"Well," Jeri said. There was a long silence. Then, "Most of my info is just hearsay that's going around the department, since Matt Johnson doesn't exactly confide in me. In fact, he doesn't speak to me unless he has to. We don't get along. But I have heard that he may be pursuing the line that Dominic was murdered and that either Dominic or you is covering up for the murderer."

"Why does he think that Dominic was murdered?"

"Crime scene investigators found some discrepancies in the position of the gun, the spent shell casing, and the gunpowder residue. It seems unlikely that the gun was in Dominic's hand when it was fired."

"Oh," I said.

"The gun did belong to him, though. Along with a good two dozen others."

"What?"

"That's right." Jeri sounded amused. "Apparently he was a gun collector. Pistols. That's what his girlfriend said. Do you know her?"

"Barbara. Yeah. She's a team roper; I'm also her vet."

"She said he kept a loaded gun in the glove compartment of his truck. She also said that everyone who knew him well knew that."

"I didn't," I said.

"I take it you didn't know him well."

"True enough," I agreed.

"Neither did I." Jeri sighed. "From what I could tell, he was a right bastard."

"A good shoer, though." I hesitated. "Am I a suspect?" I asked her.

"Hard to say what Matt's thinking," she answered crisply. "But you don't have any obvious motive. If you'd been involved with Dominic or if you stood to gain in any way by his death, that would be different."

"Who does?"

"Gain? The way I heard it was that his not inconsiderable estate and a hefty life insurance policy were made out to Dominic Castillo Jr., Sophia Castillo, and Carlos Castillo."

"Dom and Sophy are his two kids with Lee," I said slowly. "I don't know who Carlos is."

"As for people who've been involved with him," I could hear Jeri grimace over the wires, "the sky's the limit."

"Ain't that the truth. Detective Johnson was trying to pry the current gossip out of me, but I stonewalled him. For God's sake, where was I going to begin? Or end?"

"I'd be careful stonewalling Matt," Jeri warned. "He's very tenacious; he can make your life miserable."

"How much more grilling can I expect?" I asked.

"Who knows? As much as he wants to do. If I were working this case, I'd be very interested in the timeline. Where exactly everybody was at what time. It's got to be a pretty narrow window. Dominic arrives at your place and someone drives in and shoots him and leaves before you arrive? See what I mean?"

"I do," I said.

"So I imagine old Matt's liable to grill you a little more."

"I'm picturing myself as a well-done steak. Thanks, Jeri."

"You're welcome. But if I were you, I wouldn't mention my name or let on that you know anything about the investigation. It'll just piss him off."

"I get you," I said. "Thanks again,"

Setting the phone down in its cradle, I frowned at the blinking light on the answering machine. If Jeri was right, which she surely was, I was liable to spend a good deal more time closeted with Detective Johnson. Not an appealing prospect. Maybe I could stave it off a bit.

Erasing all the messages, I went back down to the barn.

Blue had just finished feeding the horses and was pouring some crumble into the barn cats' bowl. I could see the moleskin-colored Mama Cat lurking up in the brush; the tip of black Jiji's nose was just visible behind the haystack. Baxter sat in plain sight in the driveway and mewed plaintively; he was definitely the friendliest one of the family. Familiarity made me glance up into a nearby oak tree for Woodrow. Sure enough, there he was, perched on a branch. My tree-dwelling cat.

Blue followed my eyes and smiled. "It's like one of those compli-cated pictures where you're supposed to pick out so many of one kind of object. Find four cats in this barnyard."

"That's it," I agreed.

We both stepped back away from the bowl so that the cats would feel comfortable and watched them come in to eat. First Baxter, then Mama and Jiji, and last, like a puff of drifting smoke, little Woodrow.

I stared at the crime scene tape in its role as absurd backdrop to this bucolic scene. Then I looked at Blue.

"You once said that Dominic might have lied to protect his killer. Is that what you think?"

"I'm not sure." Blue watched me closely. "It seems possible."

"Why would he do that?"

"Perhaps it was someone he cared about."

"But the person had just finished shooting him in the guts."

Blue's long, slender fingers selected a hay stalk and began to twist it. Without looking up, he said, "Perhaps he felt that he deserved being shot."

"Well," I said. "That's a thought. In some ways, I think he did deserve to be shot. But I can hardly imagine that Dominic would buy into that idea."

"Men can have odd ideas of what's noble or heroic."

I considered this. "Dominic was being chivalrous? In some ways, that does sound like him. Or an idea that would appeal to him, anyway. By the way," I added, "Jeri Ward says Dominic had money, which I wouldn't have guessed, and a collection of pistols, which I might have."

I filled Blue in on my conversation with Jeri and finished up with, "And the only sure thing about it all is, I'm bound to be grilled numerous more times by that god-awful Matt Johnson."

"Poor you." Blue put his arm around my shoulders and began to walk me back up to the house. "How about I make you a drink and cook you some dinner?"

"Sounds great, but you did all the work last night."

"Doesn't mean I can't do it again. Remember, I'm trying to convince you to marry me. Once the knot's tied, all bets are off."

I laughed and gave him a quick hug. "That doesn't sound like much of an incentive. But don't worry, I haven't forgotten."

"Good. So what do you want to drink?"

"Not margaritas," I said firmly. "I know they're your favorite, but I've had them two nights in a row. Something different, something elegant."

"What sort of elegant?"

"I don't know. Something straight up and made with gin," I ad-libbed. "But not a martini."

"I've got just the thing."

Five minutes later Blue presented me with a melon-colored drink in a chilled cocktail glass. One sniff assured me that it did, indeed, contain gin, and bitters, too, or I missed my guess.

"What is it?" I asked.

"It's a Pegu."

"So, what's a Pegu?"

"Well, the original Pegu was a little bar in Rangoon, back in the days when it was the capital of Burma." Blue picked his glass up off the counter and clinked it against mine. "To you," he said and grinned. "Just try it, Stormy."

I took a sip. "Wow," I said. "That's different. Almost medicinal. I like it, though."

Blue bent his head over his glass and sniffed briefly, then took another sip. "My cocktail bible says the taste complexity is high."

"Your cocktail bible?"

"That's right. Great book. By somebody who calls himself 'the Alchemist.'"

I laughed. "A wizard with cocktails. Well, I do like this one. Thanks. It was just what I needed. The prospect of being questioned yet again by that detective is distinctly stressful. I erased all the messages he left on our machine and I don't plan to be in touch with him until I have to, but I know it will happen eventually."

Blue sighed. "Is that wise?" he asked neutrally.

I shrugged. "I don't owe the guy to bend over backwards for him.

48

He's been nothing but an ass. And answering machines screw up all the time."

Blue said nothing. Familiar with my stubbornly recalcitrant nature, he knew better than to argue.

"I'm not about to lie down like a doormat for any hostile and aggressive guy, cop or otherwise," I said firmly.

"Spoken like a true feminist."

I swirled my drink and sipped. One thing about this cocktail, it forced you to take your time with it.

"I'm not sure I'd call myself a feminist, exactly," I said. "I'm more of an individualist. I don't so much identify myself as a woman, any more than I do as a Caucasian, or a tall person, or a horse lover. I'm a combination of characteristics, like all people.

"And that's how I relate to others, I guess. I don't see a man as better or worse than a woman, though if I were hiring someone to buck hay, I'd probably hire a man. There're exceptions, of course, but generally speaking men are physically stronger than women. And, equally generally, women are less prone to the particular kind of macho asshole behavior that Detective Johnson displays."

"I'd agree with that," Blue answered reflectively. "Women are also a lot less likely to commit violent crimes."

"Good point," I agreed. I bit my lip. "Hot-tempered men are probably the most likely. Which makes me wonder."

"About what?"

"Sam Lawrence. Who is, by all accounts and my own observation, an extremely hot-tempered horse trainer."

"Does he beat on the horses?"

"Sometimes. But he's not without talent. He's more of the old-school type of horseman, likes a horse to be a little afraid of him. In some ways, it's understandable. What Sam mostly gets are spoiled backyard horses that have developed terrible, even dangerous habits.

The owners want them retrained so they can get along with them again. It's a tough job."

"I imagine."

"Sam's actually pretty good at it, but when he loses his temper, watch out. He's as likely to take it out on a human as a horse; he's lost numerous clients as well as stable help because he bawled them out."

"Has he ever done anything violent?" Blue asked.

"I heard he slugged someone just last month. A client who came on to Tracy. After he'd had a couple of drinks," I added, glancing down at the beverage in my hand.

Blue stood up. "What do you say to a simple fried rice for dinner? Something light."

"Suits me," I said.

Blue headed for the refrigerator. "Sounds like your friend Sam might be an ideal candidate for a questioning session with Detective Johnson," he said over his shoulder.

"Yeah," I said slowly. "I've got to admit you're right."

EIGHT

Monday morning began like every other Monday morning—busy. Damn busy. The receptionist read off a list of at least a dozen people who had called since we opened at eight o'clock. Sick horses, colicked horses, lame horses. And Lee Castillo wanted to float the teeth on a new horse she'd just bought.

"Did she ask for me or Jim?" I pointed at Lee's name.

"You." Nancy sounded surprised. We both knew that Lee usually used my partner as her vet.

"Give Jim the colic up in Boulder Creek and I'll take the one in Watsonville and do Lee's horse after that."

In another minute Nancy and I had finished divvying up the calls and I was back in my truck headed for the first client of the day. We need another vet to help us here, I thought, not for the first time.

Jim and I once had another vet on our staff for a brief six months last year. But John Romero had quit and moved on, and I for one didn't miss him. Perhaps this next time around Jim, with my assistance, would manage to hire someone who wasn't a closet woman-hater.

At the thought, I had to smile. Blue had called me a closet man-

51

hater the other night, and then a feminist. Sometimes life seemed to sort itself out into this odd battle of the sexes, men siding with men, women with women. I had never seen myself as part of that particular army, but there was no denying that a certain dismissive attitude on the part of an ignorant man made the hair stand up on the back of my neck.

Like Detective Johnson, for instance. Damn. My most fervent wish was to have nothing further to do with the guy. But it was a wish that was unlikely to be granted.

The thought of Detective Johnson led me to the thought of Lee Castillo and the rather peculiar fact that she had requested my services rather than Jim's. Lee had been using Jim by preference for almost twenty years. I'd seen her horses only when she had an emergency and I was the vet on call. Thus I knew her, but not well.

I had to wonder if today's call wasn't the result of Dominic's demise in my barnyard. After all, teeth that needed floating could usually wait. Perhaps Lee Castillo's curiosity couldn't.

Working my way through a minor gas colic in a broodmare in Watsonville—the horse had been brought in from a pasture and put on straight alfalfa hay, free-choice—I reassured the owner that all should be well and headed out to Lee Castillo's place in nearby Freedom.

An older ranch that had been chopped up into ten-acre parcels formed the framework of the small and not very upscale housing tract. A dirt road led the way in; Lee's property was the last one and included the original ranch house and barn, as well as various outbuildings.

Lee herself stood in front of the barn, directing what I thought were her two teenage children in the process of mucking out stalls. I parked my truck and got out.

"Gail. Good to see you." Lee pulled a pair of leather gloves off her hands and marched in my direction.

"Hello, Lee. How are you?" We shook hands, both of us, I thought, evaluating.

Lee Castillo was a striking woman. About my age—late thirties—she had prematurely gray hair that was a true silver color. It was also long and thick and shiny, usually worn, as now, in a ponytail down her back. The hair, combined with relatively unlined skin and strikingly large light brown eyes with dark lashes, created a disconcerting dissonance; Lee looked ageless—not young, not old, not middle-aged, a creature outside of time. This impression was enhanced by her tall, broad-shouldered frame, extremely fit body and direct, even hearty manner. A hard woman to categorize.

As we made the requisite small talk, I was struck, as I had been before, at what an odd pairing she and Dominic Castillo must have been. I couldn't imagine what had drawn them together.

Apparently I was right about the possible reason for this call. Lee wasted no time in coming to the point.

"I heard my ex was shot in your barnyard."

"So it seems," I said guardedly.

"I also hear that the cops are treating it as a possible murder."

"I hear that, too," I admitted.

"What do you think?" Lee demanded.

"I don't know what to think exactly," I said, wondering what Lee Castillo wanted from me. I noticed that her children had both stopped shoveling horse manure and were drifting in our direction, for all the world like my barn cats coming in to eat.

Lee caught my glance and looked over her shoulder. "You know my kids, don't you, Gail? Dom and Sophy."

"I think we've met," I said, smiling at each in turn.

Dom was a shock. No longer the pudgy teenager I'd last seen several years ago, he was instead a tall and heavily muscled young man with flat, expressionless eyes of the exact same shade as his mother's. Sophy, too, had changed—the rounded body more woman than girl, the expression on her face guarded. Neither of them smiled back at me.

"How old are you guys now?"

Dom looked down at his feet; Sophy shrugged. After a minute Lee answered. "Dom just turned nineteen; Sophy's seventeen." Once again Lee's focus shifted back to my face. "According to the paper, you found Dominic and he said something to you. What was it? Was he murdered?"

I stared at Lee. "What did you read in the paper?" I hedged.

"Just what I told you," she said impatiently. "A quote from the investigating detective. I can't remember his name. That you had found Dominic and he'd spoken to you. That was it. No mention of what he said. Just that it was being treated as a potential homicide."

"Oh," I said.

"You can't blame me for being curious," Lee said firmly.

"No, I guess not." I was aware of Dom's eyes on me as I spoke and the unnerving intensity of Sophy's stare.

Lee seemed to catch the meaning in my glance. "Kids, could you go finish up with the barn?"

Neither kid moved or spoke.

Lee shrugged. "Oh, all right. I know you guys are curious, too. Gail, don't mind them. We all want to know."

Now I was really stuck. Whatever I may have thought of Dominic Castillo, these were his children. I felt totally unequal to the task of describing his last moments in a suitable manner.

As I took a deep breath, Dom spoke for the first time. "We can handle it," he said. The gaze that accompanied the words was the implacable, slightly sullen stare of adolescence.

"They can," Lee asserted. "Dominic wasn't part of their lives. They always understood how poorly he treated me; neither one of them had anything to do with him."

I wondered. It seemed unlikely to me that these kids were as indifferent to their father as Lee seemed to think.

Taking in my hesitation, Lee spoke again. "Gail, Dominic was a shit. He ran around on me constantly when we were married, and

54

once we were divorced he reneged on the alimony and child support that he owed. And he didn't lack for money. Dom and Sophy know this. It's not surprising they didn't want anything to do with him."

"He never took an interest?" I asked.

Lee paused. Then she said forcefully, "He never lived up to his responsibilities. So, in the end, I got full custody. And none of us were interested in seeing Dominic."

I tried to find some emotion in either Dom's or Sophy's face in response to this statement. I couldn't. That steady mask of indifference so common to teenagers was firmly in place. I had the sense that no adult was likely to penetrate the façade.

I sighed. "There's not much to tell," I said finally. "Dominic said that he shot himself accidentally while he was cleaning his gun. I held his hand until the ambulance came. That was it."

For a moment no one spoke, but I could feel the ripple of shock go around the group.

"He said he shot himself," Lee repeated slowly.

"That's right."

"Then why are the cops calling it murder?"

"I'm not sure," I said honestly. "And now I've got a question for you. Do you know who Carlos Castillo is?"

"What?" Lee's jaw snapped shut as her eyes shot back to focus on mine. "How does he come into this?"

"I'm not sure," I said. "I heard the name. I was curious. Just like you," I reminded her.

"Oh," Lee said slowly. Then, "Kids, I really need you to finish up the barn. And Dom, go get that new horse so Gail can do his teeth." This time she spoke with some emphasis. After a second, Dom and Sophy moved off toward the barn.

"They're great kids, really." Lee smiled proudly at the departing backs. "Dom's my right-hand man."

"So, who's Carlos?" I asked.

"Dominic's illegitimate son," Lee snapped. "Born the same year as Dom."

I did some quick thinking. "Oh," I said.

"That's right. Born while we were still happily married, or so I thought. I didn't find out the kid existed for several more years."

"How did you find out?"

"The mother came and told me. She was fed up with Dominic by then, too. It was her idea of revenge."

"Oh," I said again.

"Right," Lee agreed. "Not pretty. That's what life with Dominic was like. There was always one woman after another."

"And eventually he left," I hazarded.

"Are you kidding?" Lee laughed. "No way would Dominic have left me. No, that wasn't his idea. He wanted to have the wife and kids and numerous girlfriends on the side. I just got tired of it."

"Oh," I said again. "And you say he had money?"

"Not when we were together," Lee huffed. "Oh no, then it was pretty much hand-to-mouth; I had to take a job as a waitress for a while. But after we were divorced, Dominic's father died and left him a great deal of money."

"But he still worked as a horseshoer?"

Lee laughed. "Dominic was as tight with money as he was promiscuous with his sexual favors. Can you believe it? He wouldn't even pay his child support. His own kids. I was always taking him to court. Or trying to, anyway. He was pretty slippery, old Dominic."

I could see Dom leading a black horse out of the barn and tried one final question on Lee. "Do you think Dominic left his money to Dom and Sophy?"

"I sure hope so. Who else did he have to leave it to?" Lee shrugged.

Carlos, apparently, I thought but didn't say. Instead I got the electric floats we used for teeth out of my truck and filled a syringe up with tranquilizer.

Dom handed the horse's leadrope to his mom and I gave them both my best professional smile.

"Let's do some dental work," I said.

NINE

I left Lee Castillo's place having successfully smoothed and leveled her black gelding's teeth, but with my mind buzzing with speculation. Detective Johnson had asked me point-blank if I knew of anyone with a motive to murder Dominic Castillo. Well, here was someone with a very obvious motive. Money. Alive, Dominic had failed to pay what Lee thought he owed her and her kids. Dead, it seemed, she believed he'd pay handsomely.

And from what Jeri Ward had told me, Lee was right. Though it sounded as though she had a surprise coming in the form of Carlos Castillo and his inheritance. But still, surely this was a good solid motive.

I worked my way through several relatively routine calls—shots and worming for a Morgan mare, a sole abscess on a Peruvian Paso, another bit of equine dentistry on an ancient gelding who was teaching a seven-year-old girl to ride. Just as I was leaving this last job, my cell phone rang.

"Gail, it's Nancy. Doug Hoffman just called to say he's bringing a horse in. He thinks it may have broken a hind leg up high. Jim's in the middle of another emergency call up in Felton. Can you come?"

"Yeah, I can. I don't have anything that's too important. Call Elaine Delgado and tell her I'll be at least an hour late to do her preg check."

"Will do."

I sighed as I hit the button to end the call. I hated broken legs. Generally speaking, a broken leg would mean I'd have to euthanize the animal. Horses were just not constructed to get by on three legs, as dogs and cats did so readily. Neither were most horses able to stand the degree of confinement and immobility necessary to heal a broken leg bone. Thus a broken leg almost always meant a death sentence.

And I knew Doug Hoffman well; more than that, I knew his horses. Doug had learned to team rope in the same time period that I had; we'd often sat together commiserating over our mistakes. I wondered which of his three nice geldings had gotten hurt.

My favorite, it turned out. My heart sank like a stone when I saw the dapple-gray horse standing on three legs in the dirt parking lot behind the clinic. Mr. Twister, a horse I'd admired for years.

"Oh, no," I said out loud as I got out of the truck. "Not Twister. What happened?"

Doug shook his head. "You're not going to believe it, Gail. He ran into my truck."

"He what?"

"I know it sounds crazy. But he literally ran into my truck."

"How'd that happen?" I asked, as I stepped forward to lay a hand on the horse's neck, slightly damp with sweat.

Doug sighed. "I keep my horses in a little five-acre field just down the road from my house. I got home late last night, after dark, and drove down to throw some hay to the horses, as usual. Opened the gate, drove my pickup into the field, and headed for the shed where I keep the hay. There wasn't any moon, so I couldn't see much, just the road right ahead of me in the headlights.

"That road takes a bend around a big tree just before it gets to the hay shed. I came around the corner and saw this horse flying straight at me at a dead run. I slammed on the brakes and came to a complete stop; I thought he was going to come right through the windshield and end up in my lap.

"He must have been blinded by the headlights." Doug shook his head again. "He locked it up at the last second and slid half under the bumper; I felt him hit the truck, but not hard. Then he ran off.

"To make a long story short, he ran on all four legs as far as I could see in the headlights, so I figured he was all right. I've got a new baby at home and my wife is pretty stressed out, so I just threw the hay out and went back to do my duty as a dad. But when I came back this morning to check, Twister was three-legged."

Twister was, indeed, standing on three legs, holding his left hind leg so that the hoof didn't touch the ground. I palpated the leg gently; nothing obvious. Just a lot of swelling around the stifle.

"Lead him a few steps," I said.

The gray horse hobbled off obediently in response to Doug's tug on the leadrope. He did, I noticed hopefully, put a little weight on the bad leg. Not much, but a little.

"I'm not sure," I told Doug, "but it looks like he might have torn up his meniscus joint. I'll need to shoot some X rays, though."

Doug nodded. I knew he was expecting this. As I pulled our largest X-ray machine out of the back room and plugged it in, I asked Doug, "How old is this horse?"

"Seven this spring." Doug shook his head heavily. "And he was just starting to be really solid. I thought he was going to be my number-one horse this year. It'll be a shame if I have to chicken him."

I stared at the gelding, who stood patiently waiting despite the fact that he was undoubtedly in a lot of pain. Pretty-headed, with a large, kind, alert eye, Twister was in all ways an appealing horse. His dapple-gray coat was icing on the cake, a color scheme as lustrous and ineffable as watered silk, or shadowed light on a still pond.

"It would be a real shame," I agreed. "He's a gentle horse, isn't he? I used to see your kids riding him."

"That's right. Gentle as can be—you can put anyone on him. And a top-notch rope horse besides."

"It always happens to the good ones, doesn't it?" I propped the heavy X-ray plates in position and took the necessary shots, Twister standing for it all like the gentleman he was.

Ten minutes later, I'd developed the X rays and studied them. Returning to Doug and his horse, I said, "The good news is that the leg's not broken."

Doug's wide smile faded as I added, "But the joint is pretty thoroughly torn; that swelling is probably due to leaking synovial fluid. He may never be a sound horse again."

"The leg might just as well be broken, then."

"No, not really. Given enough time, it's possible he'll heal up from this. I'd say he has a fifty-fifty chance."

"How long is enough time?"

"In my experience, at least a year. I've only had a couple of horses in my career with a similar injury. One of them did recover to be a riding horse after a couple of years."

"But that's not rope-horse sound." Doug looked down at the ground.

We both knew that team roping was a demanding event; only a horse in top physical condition could do the job.

"No," I agreed. "It's unlikely that he'll ever be sound enough to be a head horse."

"Put him down, then," Doug said, sadly but firmly.

"You want to euthanize him?" I was stunned. "What about your kids?"

"There's plenty of nice horses in the world. If I'm going to keep one and feed it, it's going to be a rope horse."

I stared at the man in disbelief. Despite the fact that it was an entirely practical point of view, I'd never even considered the notion that Doug would refuse to give Twister a chance.

My eyes moved back to the horse. Head down, hind leg cocked so that only the toe of his hoof touched the ground, Twister stood quietly. His silver-white face was shadowed with charcoal shadings; a sooty gray forelock hung between the steady brown eyes.

Horses are all different. Like people, they're individuals, some chicken-hearted, some courageous, some cranky, some forgiving. Like people, you can often see a horse's true nature shining right out of his eyes, can feel his spirit and sense his intentions. As I grew older, I knew that I could read horses better than I could humans, and Twister struck me as truly noble, a horse with a great heart.

Despite my eight years as a veterinarian and the many horses I'd had to euthanize, I still felt a plummeting sense of shock and pain at the thought of killing this animal here and now.

"If he rests out of it, you could sell him as a riding horse," I said hopefully to Doug.

"But that's a year or more down the road. I've got to feed him and take care of him all that time when I could be feeding a useful one. And he may never be sound."

"That's true," I had to admit.

"I don't want him to suffer," Doug said. "Let's just put him down and get it over with."

I looked at the horse one more time. Doug's decision wasn't irresponsible. But, still . . . Mr. Twister was special. I just knew it.

"Doug," I said, "would you give him to someone who'd give him a good home?"

"I guess so. But who'd want him under these conditions?"

"Me," I said slowly.

"You?"

"Yeah. I like this horse." I stroked Twister's patterned shoulder, wondering at my own choice.

"Sure." Doug smiled. "I'll give him to you. And I'll be real happy if I see you roping on him some day. That's great, Gail."

"Thanks," I said. "I'm not sure it's the smartest thing I ever did, but I've always been drawn to this guy."

Doug's grin spread right across his face as he handed me the lead-rope. "He's all yours," he said. "I'll even throw in the halter. And it's a big load off my mind." He strode towards his truck as he spoke; I had the impression that he didn't want to give me time to change my mind. "All those X rays are on you, now," he said over his shoulder, "right?"

"Right," I agreed. "The whole call's on me. Thanks, Doug." But he was already gone.

Turning back to my new horse, I stroked his neck one more time. Despite the fact that I wasn't quite sure how I would manage the logistical problems arising from his presence out at my place, I felt a deep peace at the thought that I now owned him and he wouldn't have to die.

Slowly, very slowly, I led him to a box stall and gave him some painkiller intravenously. As the stoic look faded from his eyes to be replaced with relief, I fed him a flake of alfalfa hay and filled a bucket with water.

"You're my horse now," I told him, and watched with satisfaction as he began to eat.

Somehow or other, I had been the right person in the right place and time to make this gesture. It all felt harmonious. Whatever came of it, I was glad to be here now with this horse.

A slow tear ran down my cheek; I brushed it away with the back of my hand and smoothed Mr. Twister's mane. What would it take to redeem all the suffering I routinely saw? The right person in the right place making the right gesture? I couldn't take them all home.

But still. "Compassion," I whispered to the horse. "It takes compassion. I think we'll get along just fine."

TEN

The rest of my day passed in a much more routine fashion. Saying good-bye to Mr. Twister at five o'clock, I went home to meet my new horseshoer and rearrange my corrals to accommodate a fourth horse.

Half an hour later, I was staring morosely at the only possible place to squeeze another pen into my barnyard and castigating myself as a softhearted idiot. I really didn't have room for a fourth horse. Nonetheless, I was bringing one home.

In the midst of these fruitless ruminations, Roey barked sharply. A black pickup truck pulled in my gate and bumped up the gravel drive. Tommie Harper, I hoped.

Sure enough. The truck parked itself in front of the barn and the distinctive form of Tommie Harper emerged from the driver's side.

Tommie was a big woman. At least six feet tall, by my reckoning. She had wide shoulders, wide hips, and a pretty good belly on her. Big-boned and strong-featured, with her blond hair cropped crew-cut short and a heavy leather belt encircling her jeans and boot-clad figure, Tommie looked about as butch as it was possible to appear.

I walked in her direction and got her wide, white, friendly smile. "Hello, Gail McCarthy."

"Hi, Tommie. Thanks for coming out."

We shook hands as Roey sniffed Tommie's heels. Tommie smiled again. "No problem. I'm happy to help you out of the mess Dominic left you in." Gesturing at the yellow crime scene tape, she asked, "Is that where he bought the farm?"

"Yes," I said, slightly shocked. Even for someone who was known to have disliked Dominic, it seemed a callous tone.

Tommie caught my look. "Sorry," she said, as she laid out her shoeing tools and lit her forge. "But I hated that bastard. I'm just plain glad that he's dead." She grinned at me. "Of course, I hope no one thinks I wanted it enough to shoot him. Especially that damn detective."

"Oh. Has Detective Johnson been on your case?"

"Got it in one. He was around this morning before I left for work, bothering Carla. But I think at this point he likes me better as a suspect." Her grin flashed again. "I've got a feeling Detective Johnson doesn't care for my kind."

I could imagine. "How's Carla taking it?" I asked.

"Well, she doesn't miss Dominic, that's for sure," Tommie snapped. "Dominic tormented poor Carla. He never got over the fact that she left him for me—another woman. God forbid. It was just too much for his poor, fragile male ego. He wouldn't leave Carla alone, he called her, he wrote her notes, he followed her; I swear he stalked her for years."

"He quit eventually, didn't he?" I asked. "After all, they've been divorced for a long time."

"Naw, he never really quit. Though he didn't hound us lately like he did in the beginning. But Carla still got the occasional note, or he'd come by the house when he knew I wasn't home. He never got over her." Once again the smile. "Of course, that I can understand."

I smiled back. I liked Tommie.

"Dominic hated me." She grinned cheerfully. "Now, if I was the one dead, you'd know where to look. He threatened to kill me a couple of times. I can't imagine how he resisted shooting me for all these years."

"That can't have been fun for you," I said.

"Oh, I wasn't afraid of Dominic. It was more the other way around. He'd go out of his way to avoid me; he couldn't stand to look at what Carla chose over him. And whatever trouble he was, Carla's more than worth it." Again the smile.

No doubt that Tommie was in love; to the impartial eye Carla Castillo was a plump woman in her late thirties with a flighty air, a girlish giggle, tiny, silver-rimmed spectacles, and a truly spectacular mane of long, black hair. Not someone I could imagine anyone falling in love with, though.

Probably Tommie wouldn't think much of Blue; I smiled to myself. At that moment, I saw his pickup coming through the gate. Looked like I would find out what they made of each other.

Blue parked his truck in its accustomed place and ambled in our direction, Freckles beside him. Tommie had finished her preparations and was studying Gunner's right hind foot. She paused, then turned to see who was approaching.

"Tommie, this is Blue Winter," I said. "Blue, this is Tommie Harper."

I watched as the two "guys" greeted each other. A pleasant handshake, a smile on both parts. I knew Blue well enough to be sure that he would see Tommie as an individual, and like or dislike her as such, not, as many men might have done, dismiss her because she was a lesbian.

Tommie, on the other hand, I was barely acquainted with. For all I knew, she might dismiss all men on general principles.

Apparently not. Tommie smiled at Blue as readily as she did at me; her direct blue eyes were friendly.

"You must be Gail's boyfriend," she said.

"I am," Blue agreed. "You must be our new horseshoer."

"Yep. Come to finish the job the old one left undone. Pretty dramatic way of quitting in the middle, I'd say. Now Gail, tell me how you want this horse shod."

"We've been using an egg bar shoe and a wedge pad on him. Just like the other hind foot."

"Uhmm." Tommie studied Gunner another minute, then selected a shoe from the rack in the back of her truck. Using tongs, she set the shoe in her forge to heat up.

"I wonder who killed old Dominic?" she said, as we watched the forge chug away.

"He told me the gun went off as he was cleaning it. And then he died ten minutes later," I told her.

"Is that right? Then why is that detective acting like it's a murder investigation?"

"I'm not sure," I said. "I guess he must believe that either Dominic was lying or I was. Since I know I'm telling the truth, the lie, if there was a lie, came from Dominic. But why would he do that?"

"To protect someone, maybe," Tommie said as she lifted the shoe, now red-hot, out of the forge. Using the tongs to place it on the anvil, she hammered it here and there, her motives indiscernible to an untrained eye.

Blue and I glanced at each other. "I guess that's the only possible reason," I said. "But who would he want to protect that much?"

Tommie dipped the shoe in a bucket of water to cool it, then measured it against Gunner's foot. Taking the shoe back to the anvil, she hammered some more. "His girlfriend, maybe," she said between blows.

"Why would Barbara kill him?" I asked.

"Because he's been running around on her." Tommie measured the shoe against Gunner's foot again and nodded in satisfaction.

"But they've been living together for years and from what I can tell, he always ran around on her. Why kill him now?"

Tommie shrugged, got a rasp from her truck, and began smoothing Gunner's hoof. "Hard to say. I know lots of people who hated Dominic almost as much as I did. Maybe one of them killed him."

"Who, for instance?" I asked.

"Do you know Sandy McQuire?"

"Just a little," I said. "She's a horse trainer of sorts. Gives riding lessons. Up near the summit."

"That's right. I'm her shoer. Sandy lived with Dominic for a while after Lee kicked him out. She left her husband and kids, just fell madly in love with the guy, God knows why. She lost custody of her kids, lost her job, lost her home, basically lost her whole life, all for worthless Dominic Castillo."

Tommie had gathered packing material, a wedge pad, shoeing nails, and a hammer from her truck. Laying the blend of pine tar and oakum against Gunner's hoof, she pressed the pad over it and put the shoe on top of that. Holding it all carefully in place, she began to nail.

Tap, tap, tap, the familiar rhythm of horseshoeing. As the nails were driven through the wall of the hoof, Tommie examined each one in turn. Gunner stood patiently and quietly, an old pro at being shod.

"Anyway," Tommie went on, once she was done hammering, "Dominic never would marry Sandy, even though she really wanted him to. She did everything, even had a boob job to make herself more feminine and alluring. But Dominic just ran around on her, like he did everyone else, and eventually left her to marry Carla. Sandy never got over it."

Tommie lifted Gunner's foot up onto a metal stand to clinch the nails down tight.

"Sandy talks about Dominic constantly. How he ruined her life, how her kids hated her because of him. She's still angry."

"Angry enough to kill him?"

"I couldn't say." Tommie untied Gunner from the tree and led him down the driveway a few steps, watching how he traveled. Grunting her approval, she looked back at me. "I was mad enough to kill him, but I didn't. Thought about it, talked about it, even, but I didn't do it. I don't know what it takes to push a person past that edge."

"Neither do I," I admitted. "Losing your kids might do it."

"It might," Tommie agreed. "That's why I thought of Sandy. Of course, Juanita Gomez hated Dominic just as much, and she had a better reason to kill him." Tommie grinned. "Better than me, even."

"What's that?"

"She had a kid by him, must be almost twenty years ago now. Dominic never would help her with anything, financially or otherwise. But he did tell her once that he'd left her boy some money in his will."

"Is the boy named Carlos?"

"That's right."

"Does Juanita Gomez have horses?" I asked curiously.

"Naw. I know about her because Carla told me. When Dominic was married to Carla, Juanita used to come around and try and get money out of him. But Dominic never gave her a nickel. It used to make Carla mad."

"Well, everybody seems to agree that Dominic was tight with money."

"So does he look good enough to you, Gail?" Tommie gestured at Gunner.

"Yeah, he sure does. Thanks, Tommie. What do I owe you?"

"Nothing, this time. It's on the house. Of course, I expect to be invited back."

"No problem. In six weeks, all right?"

"I'll put you on the schedule." Smiling at Blue and me in turn, she put her tools away, turned off her forge, climbed in her truck, and waved a good-bye. "Got to get home to Carla." Then she was gone.

Blue shook his head as her truck disappeared down the drive. "She seems nice," he said. "But it still strikes me funny, the notion of a woman in love with another woman."

I smiled. "A lesbian woman I know said it strikes her funny that a woman would ever choose to fall in love with anything but another woman. She thinks all of us straight gals are closet lesbians."

"And are you?" Blue asked.

"Not that I can tell. I haven't had so much as a single fantasy about a woman, let alone been tempted."

"That's a good thing."

"Of course, you never know," I teased.

Blue smiled. "I hope I can keep you happy," he said formally.

"You do. You'll make me especially happy if you'll help me move these corral panels to make a small pen over there." I pointed to a spot behind the hay barn.

"Sure. But why?"

"I'm bringing a new horse home."

Blue looked startled, as well he might. I told him the story of Mr. Twister and how I'd happened to acquire him; Blue shook his head at the conclusion.

"Gail, we barely have time to ride the horses you already own."

"I know," I agreed. "That's not lost on me. But this is a really sweet horse. What was I supposed to do?"

Blue sighed. "What you did, I guess."

"Besides, we won't be riding this guy very soon, if ever."

"So, we now have a pet horse."

"That's right. That's how I got Gunner and Plumber, you know. They were given to me because they got hurt. They recovered, given time. Twister might, too."

Blue shrugged. "It's certainly your choice."

I stared at him. "Do you mind me making a decision like that without asking you?"

"No, of course not. It's your place."

"You live here, too, and you help pay the feed bill and take care of the horses as much as I do. That gives you a say. Would you rather I didn't bring this horse home?"

I hesitated, then added, "I do realize I can't take home every horse I feel sorry for. But I fell in love with this gray horse the first time I saw him—it must be three or four years ago. I was at a roping, and he had such a nice way of working, tried so hard, really got his hind leg up under himself. He was talented, but it was more than that; he seemed so willing to try. He seemed . . ." I searched for the word and found it ". . . gallant. A truly gallant horse. I never forgot. And when I saw him today, about to be put down for lack of a chance, well . . ." I spread my hands.

Blue pulled me to him and hugged me. With his face against my hair, he said, "Stormy, I'm happy for you to bring home as many horses as you please. Just so long as you marry me and let me help support them."

I sighed, enjoying the feeling of his long arms around me. "I haven't forgotten," I said. "But I think we'd better start moving panels before it gets dark."

Blue sketched a bow. "Your wish is my command."

I punched his arm lightly. "Oh, knock it off." As we both bent to the task of lifting and shifting a heavy steel corral panel, I added, "And now I have something important to ask you."

"Ask away." Blue took a deep breath and hoisted his end of the panel upward.

"Who," I said with a grunt, "really killed Dominic Castillo?"

ELEVEN

Blue didn't speak until we had the fence panel in its new spot. "Why do you ask?" he said finally.

"Because I want to know." I said it more forcefully than I'd intended. "Look at that stupid tape. It reminds me, every day. The man died in my barn, or as good as. Everyone seems to believe he was murdered. That means someone drove in here and shot him. On my property. I want to know who it was."

I looked up at Blue. "It feels personal," I said at last. "This is my space. My garden, my home. Someone invaded it to do evil. I don't like it. I want to know who."

"Don't make a vendetta of this," Blue warned. "Leave it to the cops. This isn't about you, Gail. It's about Dominic and whoever wanted him dead."

"Whoever it was came here to do it," I said, "not incidentally causing me to become a murder suspect. I don't like it. I want to know who," I said again.

"Well, I don't have any new ideas," Blue said, after we carried another panel into its position. "Your horseshoer has a point, though. Dominic's girlfriend is the most obvious suspect."

"Barbara." I leaned against the fence, catching my breath. "I know Barbara. She's been a client of mine for years. She team ropes, and I used to see her at ropings. She's a real strong lady, has a temper. I can see her killing someone. But she's been living with Dominic for a while; she always seems able to ignore his flings. So, why kill him?"

"I don't know," Blue said. "But I've read that one's significant other is the most likely candidate for killer in the event of murder."

"Oh, great," I said, as we marched off towards the next panel.

Once it had been lugged into place, I went on, "So, let's try a new angle. Whoever killed Dominic was someone he tried to protect, despite the fact that the person shot him. Who would inspire that emotion?"

"A lover or a wife?"

"Or a child," I said.

"Good point," Blue agreed.

"And I just saw two of Dominic's children today."

"And?"

"I don't know how to describe it," I said. "They were odd. Very closed, very silent. I couldn't tell if it was just normal adolescent sulkiness or something different. And then there's this mystery kid."

I told Blue about Carlos as we hoisted up the last panel and dragged it into its resting place. Blue tightened the connecting clasps with a wrench while I fed the horses, chickens, and barn cats. When we were done, we walked up the driveway side by side, Roey and Freckles behind us.

I stopped to admire the climbing tea rose, Madame Alfred Carriere, festooning the grape stake fence that ringed my vegetable garden. Holding a blossom in one hand, I inhaled the sweet scent as I studied the color—cream flushed with mother-of-pearl; glowing yet pristine warmth.

Looking back over my shoulder, I found I could no longer see the offensive yellow tape; the barn, shaded by the western ridge, was dark, even as the rose shone in the last, long, golden light.

"It's hard to imagine a child murdering his or her father for money," I said, more or less to myself.

"But you're wondering," Blue said.

"Yeah, I'm wondering. Those kids seemed somehow off to me. And Lee's attitude—it was a little strange, too. But it's hard to picture any of these people driving up my driveway and shooting Dominic in the belly with his own gun."

"How would they have known he was here?" Blue asked.

"That's a good question. He would have to have told them. Of course, Barbara could just look at his schedule."

"There you go."

I could hear the phone ringing as we neared the house. "I'd better answer it," I told Blue. "I'm on call this week."

Sure enough, the call was for me. "A Barbara King has a colicked horse," the answering service operator reported.

"I'll be right there," I answered, and put the phone slowly back in its cradle.

"That's odd," I told Blue. "Really odd. We were just talking about Barbara and now I get a call from her. It gives me a funny feeling. But I'd better go."

"Gail, if you think there's anything wrong, let me go with you."

I shook my head. "What could be wrong? She could hardly call me out to her place to murder me. A little too obvious, don't you think? Don't worry, I'll be fine. If you want to do me a favor, just fix up some dinner I can have when I get home. Anything. Sandwiches would be fine."

"Will do." Blue kissed me briefly on the lips. "Be careful."

"I will," I said, and then it was back in the truck.

Barbara King lived only a few miles and a couple of ridges away from my home in the hills behind the little town of Corralitos. I drove to her place with my mind turning as busily as the wheels of my truck. Barbara was, as Blue had said, the most obvious suspect. Had she finally decided she'd just had enough of Dominic?

I'm not sure what I expected, but Barbara King, when I greeted her, was a shock. For one thing, she wasn't out at her barn waiting for me. Lights were on in the house, though, and Barbara answered my knock.

"Gail, come in," she said heavily.

I stared at her in consternation. Tall and slim, Barbara could not exactly be called a pretty woman; her face was a little too masculine for that. Still, with her high cheekbones, big eyes, and wide mouth, she was attractive enough at first glance, despite an overly strong, square jaw and a heavy brow line. The severely bobbed, frosted hair didn't make her appear any more feminine, nor did her rather mannish way of striding along. Nonetheless, Barbara normally had a certain well-turned-out appeal.

Not tonight. Tonight she looked an absolute wreck, her face lined and ashen, her clothes crumpled, her hair lank and greasy. Obvious tear marks streaked her cheeks and her eyes were red. I had never seen anyone who appeared more devastated.

"I had to see you, Gail," she said.

"You mean you don't have a colic?"

"No, that was a lie."

It was hard to muster up any anger, confronted with her ravaged face. "What can I do for you?" I asked quietly, though I thought I already knew.

Barbara lit a cigarette with shaking hands. "You were with Dominic before he died," she said, seeming barely able to pronounce his name. "That detective said that Dominic spoke to you."

"That's right," I said gently. "He did."

"What did he say?"

I watched Barbara closely but could see no sign of anything but natural curiosity. "That the gun went off when he was cleaning it. That it was an accident."

Tears welled up in Barbara's eyes and ran down her cheeks; the hand that held the cigarette shook. "Then why is that horrible detective acting like he thinks I murdered Dominic?"

"I don't think it's personal," I offered. "He acted like he thought I'd murdered Dominic, too."

Barbara didn't seem to hear me. "He keeps asking me if I have an alibi; I must have told him twenty times that I was taking my horse for a ride in the park. How can I prove that?"

"In the park?" I asked.

"Yeah. I exercise them in Lorene Roberts."

"Oh," I said. I was familiar with Lorene Roberts State Park; a large tract of wilderness, it covered many miles of coastal mountain range.

"How do you get in there?" I asked curiously, trying to distract her from her grief. "I thought it was off limits to horses."

"Oh, it is, theoretically. But I live near one of the parts nobody goes into much. I just ride across my neighbor's apple orchard and out his back gate and I'm on a trail that leads into the park. None of those rangers ever get up into this part."

"So you didn't see anyone?"

Barbara stubbed out the cigarette. "That's what that damn detective keeps asking me. And no, I didn't see anyone but Mountain Dave, and he's not worth anything as an alibi. No one can find him."

"Who's Mountain Dave?"

"A wild man. He lives in the park. Just keeps moving from place to place so they never catch him. Gets around on a mountain bike."

"I see what you mean. Hard to use a guy like that as an alibi."

I glanced around the room as I spoke, my eyes widening as I took in the décor. The house itself was an average sort of American tract house—ranch style, with Sheetrock walls and ceilings painted white and wall-to-wall beige carpeting—but every square inch of space seemed to be crammed full of some sort of "western" artifact. Horseshoes formed a chandelier overhead, Navajo blankets draped the furniture, saddles had been converted into end tables and lamps. And most striking of all, at least to my eyes, the walls were decorated with guns.

With pistols, actually, many of them looking quite venerable. They surrounded large items of cowboy art and were interspersed with what looked like antique shoeing tools.

Barbara followed my gaze. "That's Dominic's gun collection," she said heavily. "That detective went on and on about it. But it's perfectly legal to collect guns. Dominic never shot anyone." And she burst into tears again.

I didn't know what to say. Somehow, even in these extremes of distress, Barbara didn't seem the sort of woman who'd want to be hugged. Nor was I the sort of woman who easily proffered hugs. So I waited.

"I can't believe he's dead," Barbara sobbed. "I miss him so much. I don't know what I'm going to do."

Her pain was real; I didn't doubt it. Faced with the intensity of her grief, I had to believe she'd loved Dominic, no matter how hard it was for me to assimilate that fact.

"I'm sorry," I said gently. "I can only imagine how difficult this must be for you."

"I don't know how I can go on." Barbara swallowed another sob.

"Do you have someone who can stay with you?"

Barbara sniffed. "My sister offered."

"Can she come over now?" I asked.

"Paula lives up on Summit Road. It's half an hour away, and she's got horses to take care of just like I do. I don't like to ask."

"I think you should take her up on it," I told Barbara. "It sounds like you shouldn't be alone right now."

"You're right, Gail." Barbara used her sleeve to wipe the end of her nose. "I just keep looking at all those guns and thinking that it would be so easy to get it over with."

"Barbara," I said, "you're scaring me. Should I call Paula to come stay with you? I don't feel good about leaving you."

"No, no." She shook her head. "I'll be all right. Honestly. I got through the last two days. I'll go on. I'm kind of a drama queen, you know." Barbara flashed me a very weak echo of her normal grin. "But it is hard. Just tell me one thing—did Dominic die peacefully?" Tears welled as she spoke.

"I wasn't with him when he died," I said. "I did hold his hand until the ambulance came." Searching for some comforting words, I said, "He didn't seem distressed."

"That's good." Barbara was crying again, quietly now. Judging by her appearance, she'd been crying all day.

Before I could speak again, she got up and led me towards the door. "Go home, Gail. I'm sorry I got you out here on a fake emergency. I just had to talk to you."

"I understand," I said. "Are you sure you'll be all right?"

"I'll be fine," Barbara said softly. "As fine as I'll ever be."

I opened my mouth, but she literally pushed me out the doorway. "Go home, Gail," she said again. And shut the door behind me.

TWELVE

Tuesday morning was every bit as busy as Monday had been. I looked at my list of scheduled calls in dismay. All fourteen of them. My God. Every day more hectic than the last.

Even as I contemplated, I felt a hush go over the office and waiting room. Looking up sharply, I immediately spotted Detective Johnson striding in the office door, every inch of his bearing proclaiming non-horsey officialdom.

Mustering a smile for the benefit of staff and clients, I greeted him as if I were glad to see him. "Hello, Detective. Come into my office."

Detective Johnson didn't deign to answer, but he did follow me through my office door. "You're a difficult person to get hold of," he said brusquely.

"I am that," I agreed. "What can I do for you?"

"We need to talk."

"Well, it can't be now." I waved my list of scheduled calls airily. "I've got a full day ahead of me, just like you."

"How about this evening?"

"Don't you ever rest?" I sighed. "I'm on call this week, so there's no knowing where I'll be, but you're welcome to come by the house. Any progress on the investigation?"

"We're working on it."

"Any unbreakable alibis?"

Detective Johnson hesitated a minute and then said sharply, "No, and there's no shortage of suspects, either."

It was the most human remark he'd made yet.

"The more you look at Dominic's life, the more people there are who seem to have a possible reason to kill him. That's what I thought, too," I said sympathetically.

"Any particular person come to mind more than another?"

"No. I'm afraid not. And I really do have to go. Perhaps I'll see you this evening." I held out my hand, and for the first time in our brief relationship, if you could call it that, Detective Johnson shook it. Maybe I wasn't a suspect after all.

Turning back to my calls, I returned to the one that had piqued my interest before the detective's entrance. Sam Lawrence had a lame horse. I wondered if Detective Johnson had already been up to Summit Road to see Sam. I wondered if anyone had mentioned the rumor concerning Dominic and Tracy Lawrence to the detective. Maybe it was time to find out.

"I'll do Sam Lawrence's horse first," I said to Nancy as I passed the desk on the way out, "and then do the other calls up on Summit Road. There's three, it looks like. After that, I'll work my way back in this direction."

Summit Road was an hour away, at least in the heavy morning commute traffic. I crept slowly down the clogged freeway, thinking nostalgically of my youth, when a traffic jam in Santa Cruz County was virtually unheard of, unless it concerned tourists bound for the beach.

Things were certainly different now. All the roads crammed full with the county's many residents, on their way to work or school or play. The pace picked up a little after I left the freeway and began threading my way through the mountains.

Summit Road followed the ridgeline that separated Santa Cruz County from the Silicon Valley. A popular area with folks who wanted to live in the "country" but commuted to jobs in the city, Summit Road was lined with small horse ranches, mini-vineyards and the like. Though the area was mountainous and remote, still a long stream of traffic trailed down the two-way road; I drummed my fingers impatiently on the steering wheel.

Many minutes later I was turning onto the graveled drive that led to Sam Lawrence's training barn. A wooden sign overhead said REDWOOD RANCH.

It was an appropriate name. Tall, red-brown redwood trunks were everywhere, their dark green canopy shading the whole place. On a sunny spring morning, the light shafts slanting through were inviting, but cold, dank midwinter days at Redwood Ranch could look pretty damn dismal.

Sam was out at the barn, his short, slim figure unmistakable. Sam had red hair that curled flamboyantly back off his brow, a sharp, fine-featured face, eyes that flashed ready sparks, and a snappy, emphatic way of moving and talking. He was in no sense a restful personality.

Nevertheless, he was a good hand with a horse, and had, to my knowledge, retrained some very difficult problem animals, horses that I might have guessed to be unsalvageable. I wasn't crazy about his methods, though.

"Hi, Sam," I said as I climbed out of my truck.

"Gail." Sam sounded curt; he looked a good deal worse than that. He looked hungover, dead tired, and on the verge of some sort of nervous breakdown, all at once. His movements, as he brought a bay horse out of a stall, were jerkier and more haphazard than usual. I could have sworn his hands shook.

"Have a look at the off fore," Sam said. "I'm wondering if it's bowed."

Putting a hand on the gelding's shoulder, I ran my fingers down the leg in question.

"Whoa, Wilbur." Sam's voice was rough but not unkind; he laid a hand on the horse's neck.

Wilbur's right front was very swollen behind the cannon bone; most of the hair was scraped off as well. I thought I could feel the tendon, however, smooth and strong beneath the swelling.

"I think he's just injured the tendon sheath; it doesn't feel like he's bowed," I said, stepping back to look at the horse. He had scrapes and dings all over him, and what appeared to be rope burns on his legs. "How lame is he?" I asked.

"Not very."

Sam clucked to the bay and led him off at a trot. Wilbur did limp a little, but he looked mostly stiff and sore to me.

"What happened to him?" I asked.

Sam jerked a thumb at a blue plastic tarp lying in the nearby arena. "He was under that for a while."

"He was what?"

"Under that tarp."

"Why?"

" 'Cause the bastard needed a lesson, that's why." Sam spat what I could only assume to be tobacco juice into the dust by his feet. "He's a high-priced western pleasure horse that wouldn't quit spooking at stuff, made him worthless as a show horse. Girl brought him to me, was at her wit's end. Told her I'd fix him."

"So you put a tarp over him?" I was horrified.

"Works every time. Tied his legs together, jerked him down, put the tarp over him, and left him there for an hour. I doubt this son of a bitch will spook at anything now."

I stared at Wilbur in dismay. A breedy-looking horse, with a delicate throatlatch and a refined face, Wilbur had a neat white star between his brown eyes and a morose expression. He stood with his head down as if he ached all over.

Which he probably did. "How old is this horse?" I asked.

"Three." Sam spat again.

"Jesus, Sam." I was genuinely angry. "That's criminal. I've heard about that tarp routine and that it sometimes works to cure a really vicious stud horse or something like that, but to do it to a three-year-old because he's a little too spooky to be a show horse . . . I can't believe you'd do that."

"Gail, I've got to pay the bills. The woman who owns this horse wanted an instant de-spooking. Not six months of training."

"I don't give a damn what she wanted. That's cruel and you ought to know it." I turned my back on Sam Lawrence and poor Wilbur and marched towards my truck, as pissed as I can remember being. "Cold water and ice will help the leg. Give him absolute rest for a week and one gram of bute morning and evening for three days. I ought to turn you into the humane society," I said over my shoulder.

"You and my damn wife," Sam answered bitterly.

It was only then that I noticed Tracy Lawrence standing in the barn doorway. Tracy, in skin-tight blue jeans and a form-fitting pink T-shirt, her blond hair curling and frothing around a Barbie-doll face. Barbie-doll-featured face, anyway. Tracy's expression was not doll-like.

"You ought to call the SPCA on him, I agree." She glared at Sam even as she spoke to me.

"Somebody's got to pay the bills, Tracy, and it sure as shit ain't you."

"You're such an ass, Sam." Tracy turned her back on her husband and followed me out to my truck.

"He is, you know," she said bitterly to me.

I was not in the mood for soothing rejoinders. "It's an asshole thing to do—tie a young horse up and leave him under a tarp just for spooking."

"I know it," Tracy snapped.

"I wouldn't have thought it of Sam."

"Oh, he's just pissed off all the time now. At everything. If I so much as speak to another man, he's jealous." She gave me a sideways look, like a wary filly. "I heard Dominic Castillo was shot out at your place."

I sighed. "That's right."

"He was alive when you found him; that's what I heard."

"That's right," I said again.

Tracy glanced over her shoulder; Sam was putting Wilbur back in his stall. "Did Dominic say anything to you?" she asked.

My ears pricked up at that. "Yeah, he did."

"Did he say who killed him?"

"No."

I watched Tracy closely and saw her shoulders slump, whether from relief or disappointment I wasn't sure.

"What did he say?" she asked.

"That the gun went off while he was cleaning it. That it was an accident."

Tracy's eyes widened in surprise; once again she looked over her shoulder, checking on Sam's whereabouts. "But," she said and then stopped. Sam was staring at us from the stall doorway, his expression not pleasant at all.

Tracy clamped her mouth firmly shut. Giving me a quick smile and a wave, she turned and marched back in the direction of the house. I got in my truck and drove—leaving Redwood Ranch as quickly as was decently possible.

Whew. I was not game, I decided, to ask Sam Lawrence whether

Detective Johnson had been questioning him. I had never seen Sam look so ragged and tense with strain, had never heard him go at it with Tracy like that. And Tracy—her behavior was certainly strange.

Reminding myself that I had thirteen more calls to get through before the day was done, I resolved to find a way to bring Sam's name to Detective Johnson's attention, and tried to put the whole business out of my mind. In another minute I was pulling in the next driveway, ready to look at an old horse who wouldn't put on weight. Then it was a mare who had gone suddenly lame in the left front— this turned out to be a stone bruise—followed by a Shetland pony who had foundered on a lush pasture. I was on my way to see a case of strangles when Nancy called on my cell phone.

"Gail. Carla Castillo has a mare who's foaling and she thinks there's something wrong. The foal's not coming out."

"I'll be right there," I said. "I'm only five minutes away."

Horses tend to have their babies very quickly; any delay can be fatal. Fortunately Carla, and Tommie, lived only a few miles from the Shetland pony I'd just finished treating. Their Summit Morgan Ranch was just down the road from Sam Lawrence.

I hurried. When I pulled into the barnyard, Carla emerged from a box stall, literally wringing her hands. "Come quick, Gail."

I dashed into the stall to find the Morgan mare down on her side, straining to give birth. Lying down next to her, I encased my hand and arm in a latex glove and reached inside.

Nose, head, one front foot—where was the other foot? I reached up, up, my arm squeezed as though in a vise, until I could feel the round knob of a knee. Gently I eased the leg forward.

Even as I took hold of the two tiny hooves, paired together now, the mare gave a huge heave. In one motion, or so it seemed, the wet, dark foal slid out onto the straw. He was breathing.

"Thank God," Carla said.

Carefully I cleaned the mucus out of the foal's nostrils and checked his pulse and respiration. All seemed normal. As Carla and I watched, the mare reached around to nose him and then began to lick him clean.

Carla smiled. "She's an experienced mama," she said. "She'll take care of him. He'll be fine now. Thanks so much, Gail."

"Lucky I was close," I said.

"It sure was. This is my best broodmare."

Carla Castillo raised Morgan horses and corgi dogs. As we backed out of the box stall, we were met by the whole canine crew. Half a dozen tan-and-white corgis sniffed my ankles in a friendly fashion, impeding my progress.

Carla shooed them out of my way, her long black mane swirling as freely as the equally long wine-colored skirt that she wore. The tiny silver-rimmed spectacles remained firmly perched on her nose as she giggled, all her curves jiggling with the motion.

"Silly dogs. I thought I locked you in the house. Cody here"—she pointed at one dog, indistinguishable, as far as I was concerned, from the others—"can open the door. Clever beast."

Carla giggled again, her normal lighthearted demeanor back in place. We both leaned on the box stall door and watched Mama give Baby his first bath. All seemed entirely well.

"I saw Tommie the other night," I said.

"So she said. How sad, Gail, that poor Dominic was killed out at your place."

"Yes, it is sad," I agreed, somewhat surprised that this was the tack that Carla was taking. "Tommie told me that Dominic had been stalking you," I added, curious.

Carla looked startled. "Tommie exaggerates," she said. "Dominic never stalked me."

"Oh."

Carla was definitely flustered. "I had nothing against Dominic. Nothing at all. Neither did Tommie."

"Of course not," I agreed.

"I hope no one's said anything to make you think differently."

"No," I said. We both watched as the foal made his first effort to stand, long legs splaying wildly. Up for a second, then down in the straw again.

"He's doing fine, isn't he?" Carla smiled.

"Yep. In just a few minutes he'll be standing there nursing. I'd better go," I added. "I've got a lot of calls today."

"Thanks again, Gail." Carla barely took her eyes off the new baby as I made my exit. Still, something in her body language, an unfamiliar tension, made me wonder if she was upset.

Upset by what, I wondered. By the idea that Dominic had been stalking her? By the fact that Tommie had said this to me? I couldn't be sure.

Reminding myself once again that I was a vet, not a sleuth, I pointed my truck in the direction of the horse with strangles, and tried to concentrate on my work. Just ten more calls to go.

THIRTEEN

It turned out to be eleven. As I was finishing up with my last patient, a routine shots-and-worming, I got the call.

"Gail, Tracy Lawrence has an emergency. A horse has literally cut his throat open. She can see the jugular vein. Can you go?"

"Yes," I said wearily. I was only ten minutes from my place in Corralitos. Summit Road was, once again, a good hour away. It was six-thirty and I longed to go home. But I had no choice. I was a vet. This was my life.

Calling Blue, I asked him to feed the animals and take care of the evening chores. Then I resolutely headed back out on the freeway, trying to keep my frustration at bay.

I had hoped to bring Mr. Twister home this evening; that certainly wasn't going to happen. At the very least, I had hoped to be home by seven, with my feet up and a glass of wine in my hand. That wasn't going to happen either. Instead, I was inching down the freeway once again. Stop, go. Stop, go. Staring at brake lights.

I tried to relax, tried to let go of my need to be elsewhere, tried to enjoy the apricot and rose shades of the sunset hanging in the western sky. Still, frustration kept creeping back in.

This was one of the worst parts of my job, this constantly being on call. More and more I resented giving up so much of my private life; more and more I longed to be home with my garden and animals and Blue. Eight years into my veterinary career, I was becoming—dare I think it—a bit burned out.

I still loved the horses, I reassured myself. Loved working with them, loved being able to help them. And I could tolerate the people. It was time I begrudged. Precious time to spend with my own horses, see what was blooming in the garden, be a family with Blue and the animals.

A family with Blue. I sighed. Thoughts that had been lying patiently in wait just under the conscious surface of my busy, busy mind rose steadily into view. Blue wanted to get married. Did I? Did I want a child?

Maybe. I could feel the longing, the buried maternal instinct lifting its head. To hold a baby, to be a mother, to walk hand-in-hand with a toddling child, the center of his universe. Mama. And I was thirty-eight years old this year. If I wanted to have a baby, maybe it was time to start trying.

I could feel the tug in the other direction, too, towards freedom and independence: no strings, or groping baby hands, attached. One thing was for sure, I thought, if I ever wanted to be married, to have a mate and raise a family, Blue was the one. I couldn't imagine a man that I would admire more, desire more, feel more comfortable with.

But was it enough? Enough to trade in this life that I had found so rewarding? I had no illusions. If Blue and I married, it would be to start a family, something that was clearly on both our minds. And if I had a child, I would stay home to raise it; I would be a proper mama. As a mare raises her foal, as any mammal cares for her young, so would I do. My baby would nurse and lie next to my body at night and be carried in my arms during the day. While my child was young and needed me, I would be there.

Give up my work? Even for a while? The thought was a scary one. Still—I fiddled restlessly with the vent fans—I'd been creeping through traffic for half an hour now, with another half hour to go. It was getting dark. I was definitely getting tired of this. Maybe it was time for a break.

Oh hell. I shoved the confusing, conflicting thoughts away, wondering if Blue realized the turmoil that his proposal would cause in my heart. At this moment, I'd rather concentrate on anything else. Like Tracy Lawrence, for instance.

Tracy Lawrence, who had seemed so furious with Sam. And who had also been surprised, even shocked, when I recounted Dominic's last words.

Why? I wondered. And why was it Tracy who had called me about the injured horse, rather than Sam?

I found out half an hour later. Dusk was giving way to dark as I pulled in the Redwood Ranch driveway, my headlights showing me the barn. No humans in view, but there was a light in a nearby box stall. I walked in that direction.

Peering over the door, I saw Tracy Lawrence, tears running down her cheeks, holding the leadrope of a palomino gelding. The horse's neck was cut wide open under the throatlatch, blood staining the yellow hair, skin gaping red. I gasped, whether at the animal's injury or Tracy's expression, I couldn't say.

Tracy jumped at the sound and turned to face me. Almost unrecognizable as the cute little blond stereotype I was used to seeing, her initial expression was a mask of fury, which rapidly softened into frustration as she recognized me.

"Gail, it's you." Tears in Tracy's voice as well as on her face. "You took so long."

"I'm sorry. There wasn't anything I could do. I was in Aptos when you called, and you know what the traffic is like at this hour."

"I know. But I've been so scared. I didn't want to move this horse or leave him for a second. Look."

I looked. Sure enough, clearly visible in the gaping hole, but apparently uninjured, the jugular vein pulsed. Any nick there could be fatal.

"I'll get my stuff and stitch him up," I said.

Returning in a minute, I gave the horse a shot of tranquilizer to keep him quiet, and had Tracy steady his head as I began the delicate stitching job.

"Where's Sam?" I asked.

Tracy's eyes flashed. "I don't know. But probably down at the bar with his buddies, drinking himself under the table."

"Oh. So, what happened to this horse?"

"I haven't got a clue. It was real busy out here today, people coming and going, bringing horses, riding. Sam gave some lessons. I mostly stayed in the house, stayed out of Sam's way. He stuck his head in the door around five o'clock, said he was going to town and I was supposed to feed the horses. I flipped him off, for all the good it did. I knew he was off to get drunk, but," she shrugged, "the horses do need to be fed and I was the only one to do it.

"I found this guy like this when I went to feed him. I can't figure out how he could have got hurt in the stall. I can't see anything sharp, can't find anything with hair or blood on it."

"It's an amazingly clean cut," I said. "Perfectly smooth, no jagged edges. Like someone did it with a knife."

"But who would want to cut poor Pal's throat?"

"Who does he belong to?" I asked.

"A twelve-year-old girl. He's her show horse."

"That is weird." I was halfway done sewing the cut up. Keeping my eyes on my work, I asked the question that had been on my mind since I got here. "Tracy, are you afraid of Sam?"

Tracy's face seemed to crumple. She made a heroic effort to hold back the tears; I could see her jaw clench. "Sam's got a bad temper," she said, barely audibly.

"I know that. Do you think he would hurt you?"

"It's more than that." Tracy put her free hand over her face. "I told him last week that I was leaving him. I told him Friday morning, while he was sober, so he would understand that I meant it."

"Oh," I said. "That explains a lot."

"There's more." Tracy looked down at her boots. "I told him I was leaving him for Dominic."

"You were what?" My hands almost jerked, I was so startled. Letting my breath out slowly, I reminded myself to stay focused on my job. Carefully I brought the flaps of skin together and resumed stitching.

"You told Sam you were leaving him for Dominic?" I repeated.

"On Friday morning," Tracy said again.

"Oh my God." It was all I could do to keep from jumping again. "So you think that Sam might have . . ." My words trailed off.

Tracy was crying openly now. "Gail, I don't know what to think. I've been so scared and confused. I've cried and cried for Dominic, but I can't tell anyone about it. I never would have thought Sam could do something like that, but now, I just don't know. He seems so crazy lately.

"And I don't know what to do. Dominic's gone, I've got nowhere to go, Sam's my husband, what am I supposed to do?"

"Do you have any family?" I was almost done stitching.

"They're all back in Texas."

"Any friends you could stay with?"

"Not really. I've only been out here a year."

"I don't know what to tell you, Tracy. I think if I were you I might go back to Texas and stay with family awhile."

Tracy shook her head firmly. "I'm not doing that. I'll get by somehow. Sam wants me; he wants me to stay. I'll work around it."

"If you're afraid that Sam killed Dominic"—I put the last stitch in the palomino horse's neck—"you shouldn't stay here. Do you want to come home with me?"

That brought a weak smile to Tracy's face. "No, Gail. But thank you."

I tried one more time. "Tracy, it doesn't sound like it's a good idea for you to be here with Sam. Really."

Tracy met my eyes. For the first time I noticed, beneath the pretty-girl exterior, a flat, cynical, hopeless quality. "I'm not sure I really care," she said.

"I'm sorry." I was done with the horse; I was ready to go. Whatever Tracy's problems were, it was clear that I couldn't solve them. I gave her antibiotics and instructions for dealing with the animal and took my leave.

It was black dark as I made my way out to the truck, no moon at all. A spring breeze tossed the redwood boughs above me, sounding like surf on the beach. There was a chill in the air. I shivered.

Climbing in the cab of the pickup, I drove out through various parked horse trailers and a couple of trucks. The big white dually that Sam drove still appeared to be absent. I hoped for Tracy's sake that it would stay gone all night. And then, at last, I was headed home, towards Blue and my little house and the animals.

Not for long. To my absolute dismay, my cell phone rang just as I hit the freeway. It was the answering service operator. "Sandy McQuire has a colicked horse and needs a vet right away."

"Tell her I'll be there in ten minutes," I said resignedly. Sandy McQuire lived along Summit Road, not all that far from Sam

Lawrence. I would have to backtrack five slow miles before I reached her little stable.

What had Tommie Harper said about Sandy? That she was one of Dominic's many ex-girlfriends, and one that particularly hated him. Hell, I thought, the ground is thick with 'em. There seemed to be a woman with a motive to murder Dominic around every corner. And there were probably several dozen more that I didn't even know about.

Not, in many ways, a very nice fellow, Dominic. And yet Tracy Lawrence had decided to leave Sam for him. How had that come about? Tracy was probably half Dominic's age. Why fall for an aging horseshoer who was a known womanizer?

Well, I did know the answer to that, I reflected. Dominic could be charming. Charming and flirtatious and apparently chivalrous. Contrast that to Sam, who, even at his best moment, was still a rough-edged fireball. Tracy was probably tired of being singed and ready to be courted awhile.

But damn. Any woman with the brains of a turnip ought to be able to see that Dominic was a bad bet. Of course, I realized a second later, quite a few otherwise intelligent women had already fallen for him. It just wasn't my weakness; I didn't find handsome, flirtatious men particularly alluring. That was why I didn't get it.

Following Summit Road, I drove through dark ranks of redwood trees, around hilly, tortured curves. Houses spangled the meadows with light. Not too far to Sandy's now.

In another five minutes I was there, pulling into a bumpy driveway to arrive at a well-lit barn. Sandy McQuire stepped out to meet me.

In her thirties or early forties, Sandy was thin and trim and had the hardest face I could imagine on a woman of that age. Fine lines radiated out from steely eyes; deeper lines scored her cheeks from nose to lips. Her chin jutted out aggressively and her mouth clamped shut in a narrow seam. She had sandy-beige hair and sandy-tan skin, and all in all, Sandy seemed an appropriate name for her.

I remembered Tommie telling me that this woman had gone through a boob job to attract and attach faithless Dominic; there was certainly no sign of that now. Sandy McQuire was, as they say, a carpenter's dream. Perhaps she'd had a reverse job done. I shook her lean, sinewy hand and asked how the horse was.

"You're not going to believe it." Sandy laughed. Lighting a cigarette, she went on. "Half an hour ago he was thrashing on the ground and now he's standing there as normal as you please." She sucked in a draft of smoke and coughed. "Have a look at him."

I followed her down the barn aisle, passing box stalls filled with happily munching horses. Bays, sorrels, the occasional buckskin or gray. I wished sadly that I was munching on something myself.

Sandy stopped in front of a stall where an unremarkable dark bay horse stood chomping hay like the rest of them. Gesturing in his direction, she said, "Thirty minutes ago he was flailing around on the ground, moaning and groaning. And now the silly son of a bitch seems fine."

"Colics can be like that," I said. "He seemed to be in a lot of pain?"

"Sure looked like it."

"I'll check his pulse and respiration, make sure everything's normal, then leave you with some painkiller; you can give it to him intermuscularly if he gets painful later. Whose horse is he?"

"Barbara King's. I didn't call her, though, what with all she's been through."

I nodded. Stepping into the stall, I asked, "What is he?"

"Four-year-old colt. Prospective rope horse. Gentle as a pup. Aren't you, Leo?"

Automatically sizing Leo up as I stepped into the stall with him, I revised my impression of unremarkable. Medium-sized, medium-boned, and a solid bay, not a white hair on him, Leo had a head that was neither pretty nor homely, and a quiet, steady eye. To a non-horseman, he was just another reddish-brownish horse. But I saw the overall congruity, the near-perfect structure, good round feet, muscling that was neither too heavy nor too light. My eyes widened in appreciation.

Patting Leo's shoulder, I said over my shoulder to Sandy, "Nice-looking horse."

"He is that. Real easy to work with, real athletic, too. Barbara has a good eye."

I checked the gelding's pulse and respiration—all within the range of normal—and listened for his gut sounds, which seemed normal also. "Are you starting him for Barbara?" I asked Sandy.

"That's right. I started a couple of horses for her, must be ten years ago now. She just brought me this guy last month." Sandy laughed. "I guess she thought I did a good enough job on the last two."

"Must be," I said politely. "This colt seems fine. Sometimes sand in the gut will cause this kind of intermittent colic, or a stone can do it. I'd keep a close eye on him for a while."

Walking out to my truck, I filled a syringe with eleven cc's of banamine and gave it to Sandy. "Call me if you have any problems," I said, praying she wouldn't.

"Will do."

And then I was back in my truck, headed, at last, for home, bliss-fully unaware of the fact that trouble had begun to coalesce, like some strange brew bubbling on a stove. Things were coming together, and I was a part of them, like it or not.

FOURTEEN

Wednesday morning did not differ markedly from Tuesday, at least for the first ten minutes. I reviewed my scheduled calls, bemoaned their number, and looked up to see Detective Johnson striding through the office door. That's when things started getting different fast. The expression on the detective's face was significantly more dire than it had been the previous morning.

"We need to talk. Now," he said.

Once again, I gestured at my office door and followed Detective Johnson inside.

"Where were you, yesterday evening, between seven and nine?" he asked, as soon as the door closed behind me.

"Where was I?" Confused for a second, I rubbed my forehead. "I guess I was stitching up a horse for Tracy Lawrence? Why?" I asked, as premonition dawned.

"Tracy Lawrence was murdered last night. Shot through the head. Sometime during that window."

"My God." I sat down abruptly at my desk. I was aware that the detective was watching me narrowly, I knew that I was no doubt a suspect, but I didn't really care. "I should have made her leave," I said slowly. "I should have. Was it Sam?"

"Sam Lawrence has not been arrested," the detective said formally, as he got out a notepad and pen.

I had lost all desire to protect Sam, or anyone else for that matter. All I wanted was that the killing stop.

"Tracy told Sam she was leaving him for Dominic. Last Friday, the day Dominic was killed. Ever since then, they were at each other's throats, or that's what it looked like to me. Tracy admitted that she was somewhat afraid of Sam. I tried to get her to leave, even tried to get her to come home with me. She wouldn't. Poor Tracy."

"Why didn't you come forward with this information?"

"I meant to," I said miserably. "I meant to. I thought I might see you when I got home, you had said you might come by, but by the time I finally did get home, you'd already left. And Tracy . . ." I swallowed. "I didn't leave her place until after eight. She must have been killed right after I went."

The detective said nothing, merely nodded in an encouraging way.

"Sam wasn't home then. I remember noticing that his truck wasn't there."

"Did you see anyone?"

"No," I said. "But it was dark. There were trucks and horse trailers parked here and there in the barnyard, but I didn't see any people. That's not saying much, though. A dozen people could have been hiding there and I never would have spotted anyone." I shivered. Had Tracy's killer been lurking in that barnyard as I drove out?

"Where did you go after you left Tracy Lawrence?"

I recounted my visit to Sandy McQuire and my arrival home at ten-thirty.

"And after that you stayed home?"

"That's right." No more calls, thank God.

Detective Johnson looked down at his notes and then up into my eyes. "I'll need to ask you to come down to the office with me and make a statement."

I sighed. "I'm not surprised. I seem to have been Johnny-on-the-spot at two murders in a row." Two almost certainly connected murders, I added to myself. I just hoped that the detective would hit on some connection besides me. "Just let me tell the office staff that I'm leaving."

Ten minutes later I was seated on the passenger side of the dark green sheriff's sedan as Detective Johnson drove us downtown. I'd canceled all my calls for the day, having no idea how long this would take.

Several hours, it turned out. Once we were seated in a bare little interview room and the tape recorder had been flipped on, the detective took me through my call to Tracy Lawrence step by slow step. Next we went through my earlier call out to Redwood Ranch, and finally we recapped my discovery of Dominic Castillo in the hay barn. All in excruciating detail. It was noon by the time we were done.

Exhausted and depressed, I arrived back at the clinic in no mood to do any work. I didn't even walk into the office. Instead I hitched my truck to the spare horse trailer we kept for emergencies, gave Mr. Twister a little IV painkiller to make the trip easier for him, and loaded him up. As I expected, he hobbled gamely into the trailer on three legs and looked at me calmly.

I petted his forehead as I tied him in. "I'm taking you home, fella," I said. "To a nice place. You'll like it there."

And he seemed to. There were the usual long, rolling snorts as he greeted the other horses, the pinned ears and the sudden squeals. All routine. Each horse asserting his claim to dominance.

I put Twister in the small pen I'd made for him and promised him that once he healed up, he'd have a big corral like the others. Then I sat down on a hay bale and watched the horses for a while.

It was so soothing, like wind in the trees, or light on water. The animals pricked their ears, stared with curiosity, ambled from here to there, switched their tails, rolled in the dust, and all in all behaved like horses do. I watched them as though I couldn't get enough, like a thirsty man drinking cold water. Or a poison victim swallowing the antidote.

I watched the way the muscles moved under the shiny hair coats, the way manes and tails lifted in the breeze, the particular cadence of a relaxed walk. I especially watched the calm, interested, aware eyes, the lively and yet docile expressions. I watched until all four horses had assumed classic resting poses under the oak trees, heads a little low, one hind leg cocked. At that point I climbed off my bale and walked up the drive.

Letting Roey out of her pen, I took a tour of the garden. So much to see, and all of it a welcome contrast to the sterile gray precincts of the sheriff's office.

Every day a new rose was in bloom. Today it was the aptly named Rêve d'Or—Dream of Gold—twining through the posts of the porch and proffering butter yellow blossoms to mingle with the lavender wisteria.

And then there was the magnificently huge salvia bush called Tequila, spangled all over with firecracker red flowers. Not to mention its smaller relative, Maraschino, with blooms of exactly that hue. Pale pink jasmine and lavender heliotrope wreathed the railing of the stairway and filled the porch with their scent. An especially beloved rose draped itself alongside the chair where I usually sat; Etoile de Holland offered huge, voluptuously scented flowers—rich dark red in color, silken, full and elegant in form, always a comforting presence.

I sat in my chair and inhaled the sweet damask perfume of the rose, Roey at my feet. A hummingbird whirred through the air to perch on a branch beside me. As I quieted myself to observe, I could see tiny gray bushtits fluttering in the oak tree nearby, could hear and see a chickadee chirping as he tugged a bit of fluff free from a manzanita bush, watched a red house finch warble his song from the peak of the porch roof.

Sun shone, a little breeze flickered through the leaves. Slowly, slowly the heavy, leaden weight began to lift. Things were as they were. I couldn't change them. Tracy was dead, but Nature still sang its endless lively song. Someday I would be dead, too, but the song would go on.

As I watched, the quail clucked uneasily; my chickens squawked a warning. In another second, a bobcat stepped from the nearby brush and paused to look around. I drew in my breath and glanced down at the dog. Roey's nose was on her paws; her eyes were closed. She hadn't a clue the bobcat was there.

A young bobcat, I thought. Much smaller than some I'd seen previously, he was only a little bigger than a domestic cat, though considerably taller in the rear-end. His short, smooth coat was golden-brown, cougar color, and he had some white fur on his belly. His ears were distinctively pointed, like a lynx's, and his stubby tail twitched.

To my surprise, my flock of chickens, having spotted the bobcat, too, not only burst into louder squawks but also charged in the direction of the predator. Led by Jack, the senior rooster, the army of chickens ran screeching and flapping toward the cat.

Holding perfectly still, I waited. The bobcat stared at his potential attackers in the detached way of his kind; I fully expected him to select a victim from the herd and grab it. However, perhaps because he was young or caught by surprise, he turned tail. First walking, then trotting, he retreated from the noisy chicken attack and vanished up the hill into the brush.

I grinned. It was amazing, the things I saw out here. The animal world, like the plant world, was infinitely surprising, constantly fascinating. I could spend several lifetimes just sitting on my porch without getting bored.

Imagine seeing the chickens chase a bobcat. Of course, I reminded myself, I'd occasionally seen quail chase my domestic cats in defense of their chicks. And like the bobcat, the cats had run. The ways of Nature were mysterious and wonderful.

Looking out over the garden, I let my mind open up, allowed myself to think about things I'd been pushing away all day. What strange pattern had I been drawn into with Dominic's murder? In what sense was Nature operating here? Was I an accidental element or a pivotal point?

I had no idea why I was involved or if I really was involved at all. The whole mystery surrounding Dominic seemed to have nothing to do with me, and yet here I was virtually present at two murders, which apparently centered on Dominic Castillo. What could it possibly mean?

Like chickens chasing a bobcat, the events were inexplicable, almost unbelievable, and yet they had happened. Even if my presence was strictly a coincidence, I was, in some sense, involved. I sat in my familiar chair, on my pleasant porch, my dog at my feet, and cast my mind back on all my past interactions with Dominic. What was I missing? Nothing, absolutely nothing, came to mind. And yet the notion that I had twice coincidentally stumbled upon murders that were connected seemed equally unbelievable.

Unless . . . I sat up straight. Unless the fact that the first murder had happened in my barn was indeed chance, but my appearance at the scene of the second was not. I had been called out to Redwood Ranch, after all. To stitch up that odd cut. A cut—I took a deep breath—that looked as it if had been made with a knife. What if, in fact, it had been?

Slowly I settled back down in my chair. Gazing out over my garden and the horse corrals, I rested my eyes on the ridge to the east. A spring wind tossed the blue-green eucalyptus tree crowns so that they sparkled in the sunshine. I breathed. And I thought.

I was still sitting there thinking when Blue drove in. Roey trotted down to greet Freckles and I stood up. Stiffly, very stiffly. How long had I been sitting here, I wondered. At least a couple of hours.

Walking down the hill, I helped Blue feed the animals and filled him in on the day's sad events. We stood for a while, side by side, admiring Twister while he ate. I told Blue about my ruminations on the porch.

"And," I finished up, "I have an idea. It's not much of an idea, but it's the best I can come up with."

"What's that?" Blue asked.

"I think I was set up to be a suspect at that second murder. I think someone slashed that palomino horse's throat so that Tracy would call me out.

"Poor Tracy. My God. But Blue, I've gone over it a million times in my head, and I don't know what I could have done differently. I did try to help her," I said.

"It is very sad." Blue put his arm around my shoulders. "And I believe that you did what you could do. We can't force other people, no matter how much we want to, you know. She had to make her own choice."

"I know," I said softly.

"Do you think Sam killed her?"

"I wonder. It occurred to me that if Sam killed Dominic here at my barn, he had to have some way of finding out that Dominic was out here. The easiest way would have been to call Barbara and ask her. She would have known where Dominic was. I thought I might ask Barbara if Sam called with a question like that."

Blue said nothing, just watched me steadily.

"And," I went on, "if that's the case, and if Sam did plan on killing Tracy, then maybe he cut that horse's throat just as he left the ranch, knowing that Tracy would find it that way when she fed and that she would call me out. He must have guessed he'd be the number-one suspect if Tracy was murdered; maybe he just wanted to create another possibility."

"It makes a kind of sense," Blue said. "If anything about this whole deal makes sense. Are you going to share this with your friend the detective?"

Bending over, I picked up a stalk of hay and twirled it between my fingers. "Yes," I said finally, "you're right. That's what I'll do. I'll tell Detective Johnson what I just told you and leave him to it. He can call Barbara. That's his job, not mine. I might have done some good if I'd told him about Sam and Tracy earlier, but I didn't. This time I will." Slipping my arm through Blue's, I added, "I'll call the detective first thing in the morning, I promise. And now, maybe, just maybe, you'll make me a margarita."

"Will do, Stormy."

And we walked up the hill together.

FIFTEEN

The next day Barbara King disappeared. The first I knew of it was when Detective Johnson pulled in my driveway at seven o'clock that evening, preceded by a crescendo of barking from Roey and Freckles. I was sacked out on the couch, feet up on a stool, praying for an emergency-free evening; Blue was sautéing chicken thighs with olive oil, onions, lemon juice, and capers. The smell was intoxicating, mingling with the spring air drifting through the open windows.

Reluctantly, I dragged myself to the door and let the detective in.

He didn't bother with civilities. "Did you see Barbara King today?"

"No. Why?"

"She's gone. No one seems to know where. She didn't show up for work at noon, didn't call. Her boss says it isn't at all like her."

"Uh-oh," I said. "So you never got a chance to ask her if Sam Lawrence called her on Friday."

"Not exactly." Detective Johnson grimaced. "I didn't tell you this morning when you called, but I had already asked Barbara King if anyone had asked Dominic Castillo's whereabouts on Friday."

"And?"

The detective gave me a look, but he answered. "Three people did, apparently. Sam Lawrence was one. Lee Castillo was another. The third didn't give a name but was described as possibly either a young man or a woman with a deep voice."

"And they all asked where Dominic was?"

Detective Johnson looked down at his ubiquitous notepad. "Sam Lawrence called near the end of the day and asked where Dominic was, said he needed to see him. Barbara told him that you were Dominic's last appointment. Lee Castillo called earlier in the day and asked for a list of all Dominic's scheduled calls. Said she needed to talk to him about money he owed her. Barbara read Lee the schedule. The unknown caller phoned right before Sam, said he/she was a client with an emergency, horse had thrown a shoe and was due at a horse show the next day. Barbara told this person that Dominic was probably on his way to your place and explained where that was."

"Oh," I said. I'd forgotten all about dinner. Blue had turned off the stove and was sitting next to me.

"Lee Castillo does not deny making the phone call, but says that she saw Dominic earlier in the day while he was shoeing at a boarding stable. She says she tried to talk him into paying some child support he owed and 'got nowhere as usual,' end of quote.

"Sam Lawrence also doesn't deny that he called, but said that he never went to look for Dominic in the end, just went down to the bar."

"Sounds right," I said.

"After talking to you this morning," the detective went on, "I decided to question Barbara King again. I got up to her place about noon; no one was there. I checked at the school where she works as a teacher's aide—no show. I went back to her home several times in the afternoon, and I've just come from there now. Still no one. No horses, either."

"No horses? That's weird."

107

"Her neighbor states that a white dual-wheel pickup pulling an enclosed horse trailer drove into Barbara King's place early this morning. The neighbor thought that the truck had some kind of logo on the door panels."

"Oh," I said slowly. "Sam Lawrence drives a rig like that. And no one's seen Barbara since?"

"Apparently not. I thought I'd just ask if you'd happened to see her, Dr. McCarthy."

"Since I just happened to be right there when Dominic and Tracy were killed?"

"That, and you called me this morning with the suggestion that I talk to Barbara King."

"I can't say I blame you," I admitted, "but, fortunately, or unfortunately, depending on how you look at it, I didn't see Barbara today. I had a full day of calls and can pretty much account for every minute of my time."

Detective Johnson nodded and produced a pen. Looking down at his notepad and then back up at me, he said, "All right. Let's begin at the beginning. You left home at what time?"

Half an hour later, even the detective seemed satisfied that I hadn't had so much as twenty minutes' slack in which to murder Barbara. "Will you get in touch with me immediately if you hear of anything that pertains to Barbara King?" he asked me formally.

"Of course," I said.

"I'll leave you to your dinner."

He stood. Blue and I stood. The dogs woofed and wagged their tails simultaneously. Detective Johnson stomped out of the door.

Blue stepped over to the stove and turned it back on. I went to the refrigerator and poured us both a glass of chilled Fumé Blanc wine.

"Damn," I said. "I don't like that."

"You think Sam Lawrence killed her." Blue served sautéed chicken onto both our plates, along with rice and snow peas.

"Pretty stupid, wouldn't you think? Drive into her place in broad daylight to murder her. And why the horse trailer?" I took a swallow of white wine and started on the chicken.

"If," Blue said, "Sam killed Dominic, he got away with driving into your place in broad daylight without being noticed."

"True enough," I agreed. "This is delicious, Blue."

"It's not too bad."

We both ate in appreciative silence for a while. Finally I said, "The last time I saw Barbara, she made a comment that sounded as though she was thinking of suicide. I guess that's what's got me really worried."

"Do you think she killed herself over Dominic?"

"I don't know what to think. But there isn't any question in my mind that Barbara was truly devastated when Dominic was killed. I never saw anyone look more destroyed. And I just keep having this image of her riding off into the woods and shooting herself."

"What about her horse?"

"Maybe she'd shoot the horse first."

"Really?" Blue swallowed some wine and met my eyes.

"I can picture it. Barbara is, or was, a tough lady. She's a really effective team roper and as intensely competitive as any man I ever knew. She never seemed particularly sentimental about her horses. I've seen her beat them up pretty thoroughly for what she considered a transgression. I can imagine her shooting her horse and then herself in some kind of quixotic gesture. She did describe herself to me as a drama queen. I think somebody ought to go look in Lorene Roberts Park for her."

"Is that where you think she went?"

"She used to ride in the park. She told me. And it's sure big enough that a body could lie there for a long, long time and not be found."

"That's true enough. Not many people get up into the far reaches of that park. But what about the truck that looked like Sam Lawrence's?"

I shook my head. "Why would Sam kill Barbara?"

"Maybe he thought she knew something that would incriminate him."

"I can't imagine what it could be. And lots of horse people own white dually pickups with a logo on the side. Lee Castillo does, for one. Hers says Freedom Arabians instead of Redwood Ranch, but otherwise they look a lot alike. Not to mention, the truck and trailer might not have had anything to do with Barbara's disappearance."

"On the other hand," Blue countered, "it would be pretty easy to haul a body away in a horse trailer, and no one would be the wiser."

"True," I admitted.

We sat in silence for a minute, our dinner finished. I gave Roey and Freckles each a tiny piece of meat I'd saved for them.

"I just have this image of her riding away into the park," I said at last. "I can't get it out of my mind."

"Should we go look for her?" Blue asked. "I'm a fair tracker."

"You are?" I was surprised. "You've got all kinds of hidden talents."

"My grandpa was the county trapper. There wasn't anything he didn't know about tracking. He taught me some, though I'm not a patch on him."

My mind was already skipping ahead. "Let's try," I said. "It's a cinch no one else will. I have a feeling our friend the detective is hot on Sam's trail. And this is something we can do that won't get us in the way of the investigation or do any harm."

"It won't take long," Blue said, "to see if she rode out recently, as long as you know where she started from."

"I'm pretty sure I can figure it out. But it's too dark now. We'll have to go in the morning. That means taking time off work."

Blue shrugged one shoulder. "It's up to you, Stormy. I can take some time off if it's important to you."

I thought about it. "Maybe it is," I said at last. "I feel involved in this whole thing already, so much of it's happened around me. But I also feel passive, almost helpless. Things happen, and I seem to be a part of them, but I'm not doing anything purposeful. I think I need to do something.

"So yes," I nodded firmly. "Let's take Friday off and look for Barbara."

SIXTEEN

Blue and I drove up Rider Road at nine in the morning. The apple orchard at the top of the hill was in full bloom, the twisted gray limbs covered with rose-tinted white flowers, a flock of butterflies. Even this early in the day, the air was heady with scent.

I took a deep breath as I stepped out of the truck. "I think I love the scent of apple blossom the most of any flower smell," I said appreciatively. "Of course, I say that about all kinds of things when I'm smelling them. Wisteria, my favorite roses, sweet peas, jonquils, lupine, elderberry, even the basil and cilantro in the vegetable garden."

Blue laughed. "You've got lots of favorite smells."

"True enough. Let's not forget onions simmering in olive oil. But this," I breathed in again, "it's so clean. Kind of spicy and fresh, almost like laundry in the sun."

Blue laughed again. "I agree with you. It is wonderful. Now, which way do we go?"

I pointed through the orchard. "Barbara lives down that way. You can't see her place from here. But, the way she put it, I think she usually rides right across this orchard and comes out on a trail over there." I gestured at the redwood forest on the far side of the orchard. "So we just have to poke around in that direction looking for the trail."

Blue glanced up and down. "I don't see any 'No Trespassing' signs."

"If we meet the owner, we can just pretend to be a courting couple. Surely he'll be sympathetic." I grinned.

Blue put an arm around my shoulders. "We *are* a courting couple. I hope you haven't forgotten, under the influence of all this investigating."

"I haven't forgotten," I assured him. "Why don't you prove to me what a mighty tracker you are? Sure way to win my heart."

"You're on."

Starting off across the orchard, I was conscious of a feeling of something not right. Something missing. "It feels weird to be here without the dogs," I said. "No dogs, no horses—I feel naked."

"I wish. What a sight you'd be, striding through this orchard like some sort of pagan goddess."

I laughed and punched him lightly in the shoulder. "You know what I mean."

"I do. But dogs wouldn't be an asset on this expedition. Nor horses."

"I know. But I miss 'em."

"Me, too." Blue smiled. "They're our little family, aren't they?"

I nodded. Almost without volition, my mind presented me with an image. Blue and I and the two dogs and a little child, all running happily across this orchard. Our child. A family.

"Here's where we need to start looking," I said roughly. "Right here along the edge of the orchard."

It didn't take long. Blue walked maybe fifty feet, half bent over, peering at the ground, and then pointed. "Here's the trail."

I stood next to him and looked where he pointed. The orchard ground, which had been rototilled at some point this spring, showed the obvious dusty battering of hoofprints. A well-worn trail led off between the redwoods to our left.

Blue squatted and stared at the crumbly dirt in front of him, then reached out and gently touched a spot with his index finger.

Standing back up, he said, "I think someone rode this way yesterday. No one's been along it this morning; the dew's unbroken. But the most recent tracks are pretty fresh. Yesterday morning would be about right."

I followed him into the redwood grove, watched him bend and stoop and peer and occasionally brush the dust with his hand. I was careful to walk outside the main body of the trail, treading only on the redwood duff alongside.

Periodically Blue would make a comment. "Deer crossed here," or "See that coon," and I would look and register the track. Ten minutes of slow reconnoiter later, we emerged from the redwoods into a scrubby meadow. The trail was a smooth, dusty stripe between grassy banks.

"Ah," Blue said, and spent a good long time examining a wide spot. Finally he spoke. "I'm pretty sure two separate shod horses came through here yesterday. One with bigger feet than the other. The smaller-footed horse had half-round shoes in front and squared toes behind."

"Oh," I said. "Two horses, hmm."

"So what now?" Blue asked.

"Follow them, I guess. See where they went."

On we went. Blue kept his eyes on the ground while I tried to imagine what two horses could possibly mean.

"They came through here at about the same time. One right behind the other, or right next to him, at times," Blue said over his shoulder.

As if, I thought, someone had ridden behind Barbara, or beside her, possibly pointing a gun at her. The image made me shudder; I glanced over my own shoulder quickly. Once again we were in the forest; I felt as if the trees were watching me.

Dim and shadowy, the redwoods stretched high to form a lacy green canopy far above. The understory was leafy with bay trees and tangled vines, the floor carpeted with trilliums. All lush, almost tropical in exuberant growth, all hushed with the eerie quiet that takes hold in a mature redwood grove.

I could see sunshine through the trees ahead; it looked like another little meadow. Picking up the pace, I hurried forward, almost tripping over Blue when he bent to study the ground.

"Where are you off to in such a hurry?" He smiled up at me.

"Out of the trees." I shivered. "It's cold underneath here, for one thing, and for another, I'm getting the creeps. I feel like the trees have eyes."

"Redwood forests are different, aren't they?" Blue stood up. "Very hushed, like a church."

Then we were out in the sunshine again, surrounded by dusty grass and wild sweet peas. Blue stooped to study the ground and nodded. "The same two horses. So, how long do you want to track them for, Stormy?"

"As long as we can stand it, I guess. I want to know where they went."

On we went. And on. Uphill and downhill, mostly we seemed to be following the coastal ridge. Our trail led steadily northward. Occasional paths branching off to the side caused Blue to bend and examine the dirt, but our two horses stayed on the main trail.

An hour or so later, our trail fed into a dirt road, running east/west. After some study, Blue said, "The horses went east. This looks like the main fire road that crosses Lorene Roberts Park. I used to ride my mountain bike up here."

"I didn't know you were a mountain bike rider."

"That was a few years ago." Blue was headed down the road, his eyes cast down before him.

"Barbara said she ran into some crazy guy on a mountain bike the last time she was riding in here. The day Dominic was killed. She said the guy was worthless as an alibi because no one could find him. She called him Mountain Dave."

Blue laughed; the sound seemed to echo through the quiet woods. "I know Mountain Dave. He's sort of a local legend."

"He is? Who is he?"

"That's hard to say. No one seems to know where he came from or have any more names for him than Mountain Dave. He lives up in this park and rides his mountain bike to get around. Moves his camp all the time; the rangers have never caught him. He knows this whole park like you know your own property. Every once in a while he'll show up at a mountain bike race, what they call cycle cross, and just beat the socks off all the high-end riders. It's pretty funny; the pros will be decked out in fancy cycling duds and riding expensive bikes, and here comes Dave in jeans and a T-shirt on a beat-up old cycle and just cleans their clocks."

"He sounds like quite the character."

"He is that."

"Is he crazy?"

"Oh no," Blue said. "He's an iconoclast."

The fire road proved more difficult as a tracking medium. Blue was forced to stop often. At one point, he stared awhile and then motioned me over. "See that?" he asked.

"What am I looking for?"

Blue pointed to a narrow, patterned line through the dust. "That's a bike track. And if you look, you'll see that it runs right over the track of our smaller-footed horse. So the bike came through after the horse did. It was sometime yesterday, because, as you can see, the dew isn't disturbed. If I had to guess, I'd say the bike might have been fairly close behind our horses, at this point."

On we went. Some time later, Blue stopped again. "Look," he said. "The bike overtook the horses right here. See where it went by. And here," he walked ahead, "the horses came through after the bike. Here's a hoofprint on top of the bike's trail."

"So the bike rider saw Barbara and whoever was with her. At least, we assume it was Barbara."

"That's right. It doesn't look as if the cyclist stopped; there's no track of a foot on the ground, or any break in the line of the tire track. The horses moved over to let the bike by, and whoever the cyclist was, he certainly saw our horsemen."

"Onward," I said wearily. "Let's see where they went."

Blue marched on, pausing from time to time to examine the road. I trudged behind him. The sun climbed steadily through the sky and the air warmed. I took off my sweatshirt and tied it around my waist.

What seemed like miles and hours later, the fire road dipped down into a canyon. Mixed forest here, tanbark oaks and sycamores mingled their palmate leaves with the occasional redwood.

Straight overhead, sun poured down with considerable strength. Little puffs of dust rose with every footfall and the air smelled sweetly of tanbark and pollen.

Sweaty and sore as I was, I still gasped with delight as the creek came into view. "Oh, Blue, look," I said.

Surely no grand estate ever boasted a more beautiful and harmonious water garden. Our road descended in graceful loops to a delicately arched bridge spanning a boulder-strewn stream. The water chattered; pools and rills and little falls arranged themselves in perfect, balanced cadence; ferns and vines wreathed clear eddies of still water. Wild iris and trillium clung to the banks; maples fluttered leaves like waving hands in the cool air.

I stared in bemusement; had the architect of this bridge really planned that gentle arch and the slender railings to resemble Claude Monet's Japanese bridge at Giverny, or was it just a happy bureaucratic accident? I inclined to the latter view, given my experiences of govermental agencies, the state parks department included. But even if the design was orchestrated, no foresight could have predicted just this particular branch above the water, or the mysterious mossy stones that outlined the deep downstream pool. It was a fortuitous chance—Nature's choice—like virtually every happy incident in my own garden.

"Wow." I took a deep breath. "That is really beautiful. And I am really thirsty."

Blue and I hurried forward, both of us scrambling down the trail that led to the water. Blue paused to examine the bank and said, "Our two horses drank here."

"Me, too," I said. "This creek ought to be fine, as far into the woods as we are."

A voice replied, "It won't hurt you. I drink it all the time."

Not Blue's voice. A strange voice, coming from where? I stared wildly around but saw no one.

Blue smiled. I followed his gaze with my own eyes. Under the bridge. A man, sitting cross-legged in the deep shade under the bridge.

"Hi, Dave," Blue said.

SEVENTEEN

Do I know you?" The stranger got to his feet.

"Not really," Blue replied. "My name's Blue Winter. I used to ride bikes. I've seen you around."

Was this really the legendary Mountain Dave? I could see the shape of a bicycle resting near his feet.

The man who emerged from under the bridge looked like no human being I'd ever seen before. He wore only a pair of battered cut-off jeans; torso, legs, and arms were uniformly brown. Muscles bulged under taut skin; sinews and veins were prominent. Long, shiny brown hair was tied back in a ponytail; an equally long, shiny beard streamed down his chest. He was possibly the fittest-looking hermit on the planet.

"I recognize you," he said slowly to Blue. "Big, tall, redheaded guy on a bike."

"That was me," Blue agreed.

Dave smiled, a flash of white teeth framed in dark hair.

"This is Gail McCarthy," Blue added.

"Nice to meet you," I said.

Dave nodded. "What brings you so far into the park?"

"We're tracking some horses," I said.

Dave nodded again. "Uh-huh."

"Have you happened to run across them?" Blue asked.

"When?"

"Yesterday."

"I don't think so." Dave shook his head. "I don't keep much track of time, or days, but I don't think I saw any horses yesterday. You don't see many horses in this park. Against the rules." Again I saw the teeth, white in the dark brown beard.

"I think one of the riders was a woman," I offered, "with short, grayish-blond hair. I don't know about the other one. The woman, her name's Barbara, mentioned you. She knows who you are."

Dave nodded. "I know who she is, too. She rides in here once in a while. Comes from Rider Road."

"That's right. Did you happen to see her out riding last Friday?" I asked.

Dave shrugged. "I couldn't really say. I don't pay a whole lot of attention to what day it is. I've seen her in here not too long ago, but I don't know exactly when."

"Oh," I said.

"A cyclist passed these horses yesterday," Blue said. "Maybe a couple of miles back."

"That was probably John."

"John?" Blue asked.

"Yeah. His name's John. He's a cycle cross nut; he's always training. He rides across the park a lot. Starts down in Aptos and comes out near the summit. His wife picks him up. Not too many people get into this part of the park, but I see John's tracks a lot."

"Skinny, knobby tires?" Blue asked.

"Yep. Cycle cross bike."

"Do you know how to get hold of him?" I asked. "It would be great if we could find out what he saw."

Dave gave me a long, steady look. "Why are you so interested in these horses?"

"Barbara's disappeared," I said. "There's a possibility she's dead."

Dave regarded me for a while, then nodded imperceptibly. "I don't know John's last name, let alone his phone number. But I'll see him again; I always do. If you give me your phone number, I'll ask him to call you." And, to my surprise, he pulled a notepad and a stub of a pencil out of the pocket of his shorts.

Giving him my name and phone number, I asked, "Where are you headed?"

"East, on the fire road. I just came down the back trail from the top of Mount Rosalia." He waved his hand at what looked like a veritable deer track leading up the sidehill.

"Wow," I said. "You came down that on a bike?"

Dave and Blue laughed, almost in unison.

"Dave's a master," Blue said kindly. "I imagine he could come down that trail in his sleep."

I smiled. "If you're going east, would it be too much to ask you to see where these horses went? I have to admit I'm getting tired, and we've got three or four hours' hike ahead of us just to get back to where we started."

Dave considered this a moment. "I can do that," he said at last. "Don't have anything else I need to do. Just ride. I've got your phone number. I'll tell you where they went. Though I might not get around to calling for a day or two."

"That's fine," I said. I was weary to the bone and inexpressibly relieved to have discovered a graceful way of giving up the pursuit. Following Barbara suddenly seemed a lot less important than finding something to eat.

"Thank you." Blue and I got out the words at the same time.

"No problem." Dave was already mounting his bike. "I'll be in touch."

And then he was off, his bike clambering up the steep trail to the fire road as if its tires were hooves, propelled by those sinewy, driving legs. In two seconds, he was gone.

"He's amazing," Blue said admiringly. "You should see him ride in a race sometime. There's no one like him. All he does is ride that bike."

"Nice work, if you can get it," I agreed. Bending down, I began scooping and slurping water. Between gulps, I said, "Blue, I'm beat. I know this was my idea and I'm sorry to give up on you, but I don't want to go any farther."

"Hey, Stormy." Blue knelt down beside me. "Not to worry. I'm tired, too. We'll go home."

And he raised cupped hands full of clear water to my lips.

EIGHTEEN

I woke up Saturday morning aching all over. Holding perfectly still, I assessed the pain. Sore thighs, sore calves, sore muscles everywhere. Nothing else. Ankles, knees, joints . . . all were fine. I wasn't injured; I was just severely out of shape.

Lying next to Blue in a warm cocoon of blankets, I remembered yesterday's long slog out in excruciating detail. Without the motivation of pursuit, the miles and hills had seemed endless. My pace had lagged until I was barely trudging along.

Patiently, Blue had waited, had encouraged, had playfully pushed me up the steepest hills. And then, later, the ordeal behind us, had taken me to a nice dinner at a restaurant perched on the cliffs overlooking the bay.

And now, here I was, safe and warm, albeit sore, in his arms. I have a good life, I thought, not for the first time.

I could hear a faint, rhythmic whisper; squinting out at the grayish light that filtered through my uncurtained window, I recognized a change in the weather. Rain, pattering gently on the tin roof, a delicate, silvery tracing of vertical lines in the misty air. Soft spring rain. Good for the garden, good for the earth.

Rolling over, I sighed with contentment. It was Saturday; with any luck at all, I could lie here awhile and listen to the rain and Blue's steady breathing.

Wrong. Not a minute later, like a voice from hell, came the shrill, insistent bleat of the phone. Grabbing the receiver, I answered quickly, so as not to wake Blue.

"Dr. McCarthy, I have a colicked horse in Watsonville."

Naturally, it was the answering service. I was, of course, on call. I took directions and a name and hung up.

Blue blinked at me sleepily.

"I have to go," I said.

"Too bad."

"Yes, it sure is. I'll feed the horses on my way out. Sleep awhile."

"Thanks, I'll do that."

Rolling out of bed, I avoided Blue's long legs and the two sleeping dogs. Jeans and a sweatshirt and boots, a quick pot of coffee brewing, a perfunctory comb through the hair, a flake of hay to each of the four horses, and I was in the truck, coffee cup in hand, rain pattering softly on my windshield.

The pickup bumped and jolted over the numerous potholes and ruts in my imperfectly graveled drive, nearly spilling the coffee all over my lap. Not for the first time I reminded myself to hire a tractor and dump truck to scrape and add fresh base rock to my road. The long grass along the verge needed mowing, too, as soon as the daffodils died down.

If it wasn't one thing it was another—the constant lament of the gentleman (or in this case, gentlewoman) farmer. With a full-time job to occupy my time, I could never keep up on the garden and barnyard chores. And now, to top it off, I had been cast into the middle of a murder investigation.

Automatically my mind went back to yesterday. What had it meant? Two horses had ridden out from Barbara's direction on Thursday morning. Was Barbara even now lying dead in some gully?

You're losing it, Gail, the more pragmatic part of my mind admonished. For all you know, those two horses didn't even come from Barbara's place. Maybe Barbara's safely at home right now, snoozing away. Why do you have this bee in your bonnet, this obsessive fancy that she disappeared into Lorene Roberts Park, never to be seen again? What about the truck and trailer the neighbor saw?

And why repose so much confidence in Mountain Dave? You trusted him with the outcome of your search without a second thought.

I sighed out loud and sipped some coffee. Logical mind was right, in a way. I couldn't really defend my intuition. I had trusted Mountain Dave more or less instantly, and I did believe that Barbara had ridden one of the horses we tracked.

But that was as far as it went. I hadn't a clue what to do next, hadn't any ideas at all, really, except to wait.

Wait for what? I asked myself in annoyance.

You'll see; I could swear I heard the amused answer.

Good God, I really was losing it. Not only did I have an inexplicable, intuitive version of blind faith, I was now hearing voices in my head. Not good.

Driving south on Highway 1, I could see the big sweep of the Monterey Bay visible in front of me. Where exactly was I going, anyway? Time to get my mind back on the job. I glanced at the hastily scrawled directions on the seat beside me.

Exiting the freeway, I made my way down narrow farm roads, through fields of agricultural land. Several right and left turns later, I crossed a bridge over the Pajaro River, and took a bumpy dirt road that followed the levee. Two miles through fields of artichokes, empty except for wheeling seagulls, brought me to a small farmhouse

125

with a barn behind it. I could see a sorrel horse in the corral next to the barn; no human beings were visible.

The gentle rain still splattered down; there was coffee in my cup. I took another sip and stared out my windshield. I'd never been here before, and the house and barnyard looked nearly derelict. Still, there was a horse in view, though he showed no obvious signs of being colicked. Where was the client?

I glanced at my note. Paul Thorne, it said. I hoped Paul Thorne would be reasonably punctual.

He was. I had just settled myself comfortably in the cab of the truck when I noticed the black car creeping down the road I'd arrived on. A black BMW, which was odd. Judging by the house and barn, I would have expected a battered pickup.

The BMW advanced towards me—slowly. The potholes in that road were probably making the driver curse. Eventually the car reached the barnyard and rolled to a stop a little way from my truck.

A man got out. Not someone I recognized, and yet he looked strangely familiar. A young man, with dark hair and olive skin, a handsome, high-cheekboned face. The black turtleneck and gray slacks he wore looked as out of place in this barnyard as his shiny, lowered black car. He stared at my truck and waited.

Now what? I did not like the look of this man, of the whole situation. Still, this was my job. He was probably just some wealthy farmer who favored the big-city look on his day off. He'd called me about a colicked horse; I could hardly run away because I didn't care for his appearance.

Picking my cell phone up off the seat, I dialed my home phone number. With the phone in my hand, held close to my mouth, I got slowly out of my truck.

"Hello, Dr. McCarthy." The voice was lightly accented.

"Hello," I said. "Are you Paul Thorne?"

"I called you out, yes."

"For a colicked horse?"

"That is so."

I could hear the phone ringing in my ear, but Blue wasn't picking up. He must be outside. I hesitated, and in that second Paul Thorne moved towards me—fast.

Before I could react, the phone was jerked out of my grasp; a long, slim finger pushed the "end" button.

"What the hell?" I turned and leaped for my truck.

"Stop."

Something in the icy tone froze me. Slowly, I looked back over my shoulder.

Yes, there was the gun. In his hand, pointing right at me.

My heart jolted violently; I could feel it thudding—great, wrenching beats. Gasping, I reached out to lean on the pickup, almost physically sick from the rush of adrenaline into my blood.

Paul Thorne spoke quietly. "I need to talk to you, Dr. McCarthy. And I don't want you to call anyone on your little phone."

"It won't help," I said weakly. "I told my boyfriend where I was going; I was just talking to him before you drove in, telling him how odd this place looked. That was him calling me back. If I don't answer, he'll call the police."

Paul Thorne's dark eyes studied me impassively. Despite his youth, the impression of menace was convincingly real. "I think not," he said. And then, "Dr. McCarthy, I must speak with you. It would be best if you cooperated."

For a long moment we looked at each other. I don't know what he saw, but those brown eyes were as cold and implacable as glacier ice.

I lifted my chin. "What do you want to talk about?"

"My father."

"Your father?"

"That's right. Haven't you guessed? I am Carlos Castillo. I am said to look very like my father."

"Yes," I said. "I guess you do. Why are you pointing that gun at me?"

"It is necessary that you stay here and that you do not call anyone on the phone. I will explain. As I said, I need to talk to you."

"So talk. I'm getting wet." I put as much bravado into my tone as I could muster over my pounding heart.

"You were with my father before he died. He spoke to you."

"That's right."

"What did he say?"

"That he shot himself while cleaning his pistol. That it was an accident."

"He did not mention my name?"

"No, why?"

"I have my reasons for asking, but I would not expect you to believe them. Still, I need to know. My father has left me a great deal of money."

"So I hear." Little beads of water were coalescing in my hair and dripping down my forehead.

"I work with some people whose names you would not know. These people are, shall we say, at odds with me right now. They believe that I owe them some money. I do not agree. At one time I foolishly told them that when my father died I would inheirit much. Now I find that my father has been murdered, and my former business partners are demanding their money. It makes me wonder." Carlos Castillo said it quietly; the words still resonated with some force.

"I am wondering if my father said anything, or perhaps there was something you noticed, anything at all. I am wondering if this murder can concern me."

"That I believe." I waited. Carlos Castillo watched me with opaque eyes. The silence grew.

"Are you sure there is nothing else you remember?"

"I'm sure," I said.

"Do not think that I killed my father."

I flinched. This was exactly what I was thinking. It seemed to me that the story about his business partners might be just that—a story—told to cover up his real reason for calling me out here. Which was more likely to find out if Dominic had named Carlos as his killer.

"My father and I had not spoken in years. He would not help my mother when we needed his help. For some time now, my mother and I have not needed anything from him. I have taken care of it. I do not need my father's money. And then," he spread his hands, "comes this business. As I say, I am very curious."

I said nothing. I could think of nothing whatsoever to say. My gut was clenched so tightly it was hard to get any words out, anyway.

"I am a man who has nothing to do with the police." The voice was soft and even. "I must ask you not to repeat this conversation to them, and not to mention my name. I am a truly dangerous man, Dr. McCarthy. You should heed this warning."

"I believe that, too. I won't talk to the police." I was having a hard time speaking; any attempt at bravado was over.

"Do not mention this place, either," Carlos went on. "It belongs to a friend of mine who also does not care for police."

"Not a problem," I said weakly.

"I have no wish to harm you," he said after a moment. "You may go." One hand tossed the cell phone in my direction.

I caught it. Without a backward glance, I climbed into the cab of my truck, not too slow but not too fast either. Carlos Castillo got back in his car. I started my truck and drove out, the black BMW a sedate distance behind me.

I watched him in my rearview mirror all the way back to the freeway entrance, where his car took the turnoff toward downtown Watsonville. Without thinking about it, I pointed the truck's nose for home, taking the freeway on-ramp, running, as a frightened animal will do, for my den.

I believed that Carlos Castillo was a truly dangerous man, just as he'd said. His veiled threat was far more intimidating than any amount of bombast. I recognized the professional criminal under the smooth veneer; he would shoot me if I threatened him, without mercy or much thought.

My guts twisted and rolled; I realized my hands were clenching the steering wheel so tightly they were getting numb. I loosened them, stretched my fingers, unlocked my jaw. Faced the fact. I was scared shitless.

NINETEEN

I told Blue. What else could I do? I could hardly hide my fear from him; one look at my face as I got out of the truck and he was by my side.

"What happened, Gail?"

So I told him. "And I am not, I am absolutely not, going to tell the police anything," I said. "Don't try to convince me."

"All right. I won't." Blue squeezed my shoulders reassuringly. "This man has no reason to harm you. You haven't done him any harm."

"Do you think he killed Dominic? Or his so-called business partners did?"

"Hard to say," Blue answered. "It's clear you believe he was capable of it."

"Yes," I said emphatically. "Definitely yes. And I believe he could have been involved with the sort of people who might have done it without a second thought. But why kill Tracy?"

"Maybe they were two separate crimes, with different killers."

"Oh," I said. "Carlos or his friends killed Dominic and Sam killed Tracy. Is that what you think?"

"Stormy, I'm not sure I think anything, except that you're getting way too involved in this."

"Blue, what the hell can I do? Do you think I wanted to be right there when those two people were killed? Do you think I arranged for Carlos to threaten me?"

"No, of course not. I'm sorry. I just want you to stay safe."

"I'm sorry, too." I hugged him. "I'm just upset."

"Who wouldn't be?"

We both heard the phone ring at the same time. "Oh no," I said.

But it wasn't the answering service. It was Jeri Ward. "Thought you'd like to know, Gail. Matt Johnson found the gun that killed Tracy in Sam's tack room under a pile of old saddle blankets."

"With Sam's fingerprints?"

"No prints at all. Wiped clean. Same as the gun that killed Dominic. Pretty much every idiot knows enough to do that these days."

"Has Sam been arrested?" I asked.

"Not yet," Jeri said crisply. "The evidence is just circumstantial. But I think Matt's close."

"Has Barbara King been found?"

"No. No one's seen her since she disappeared on Thursday. You've got to wonder."

"Yeah," I said, "you do."

"How many horses did she have? Do you know?" Jeri asked.

"Two or three, I think. One of them's a real flashy black-and-white paint. It's been a while since she called me out to do any work. I can't really remember the others."

"It just seems odd that all her horses disappeared, too."

"Yeah," I said. I was feeling overwhelmed. I simply could not reconcile all the things I knew. I thanked Jeri for informing me, hung up the phone, and turned to Blue.

"They found the gun that killed Tracy," I said, and repeated what Jeri had just told me.

"So how does Carlos Castillo fit in?" Blue said ruminatively, once I was done. "Why did he want to know what Dominic said?"

"Maybe he was wondering if Dominic accused him? Blue, this guy was creepy. So young and so polished. I had the gut feeling he's probably killed several people in his short life."

"He struck you as a professional criminal?"

"Oh yeah. I'd guess some kind of drug baron. Something that makes money. I believed him when he said he didn't need money."

"In these parts, it could be fighting chickens," Blue said.

"Fighting chickens? I thought that was a poor man's sport."

"Not anymore. The police raided a place near where I work, confiscated thirty thousand dollars."

"Wow."

"So, yes, your friend Carlos could be making good money on fighting chickens. But why would he kill Dominic?"

"I really have no idea. Revenge for the way his father treated him, maybe. Or maybe Carlos does need a big sum of money right now—to pay off his partners in crime. Maybe that part of his story was true. If it was Carlos, it would explain why Dominic covered up for him—his own son and all. Maybe Carlos was the unknown person who called Barbara to find out where Dominic was. It was a young man's voice, the detective said."

"Yeah," Blue said slowly. "Or a woman with a deep voice. Which rather accurately describes your new horseshoer."

"Tommie," I said. "I forgot all about Tommie. And Lee's son, Dom, is a young man, too. It could have been any of them."

"Or someone whose horse threw a shoe," Blue reminded me.

"Maybe. But Dominic died. Someone drove out here and shot him. And now Tracy's dead, and Barbara may be dead, too."

"Do you still think Barbara rode into Lorene Roberts and shot herself?" Blue asked.

"I don't know what to think anymore. The fact that there were two horses makes me wonder if someone rode in there with her. I wish Mountain Dave would call and tell us where they went."

"Maybe the horses didn't come from Barbara's place," Blue said. "We didn't track them out of her barnyard. Maybe she's got neighbors who ride across that orchard and into the park, too."

"She very well may have," I agreed. "Oh Blue, I'm really confused."

Blue put a comforting arm around my shoulders and hugged me. "It isn't up to you to solve this, Stormy. Maybe our friend the detective already has."

"So Sam killed Dominic because of Tracy, and then he killed Tracy, and finally he killed Barbara because she knew something that would incriminate him, and hauled her body away in the horse trailer. Or," I said, "maybe Sam killed Dominic and Tracy, and Barbara killed herself. Or lost herself."

"Lost herself? What do you mean?" Blue looked down into my face.

"Lorene Roberts is huge," I said slowly, "and nobody gets back in there much. People get lost. I was driving down Eureka Canyon one morning on the way to my first call of the day when I saw a girl walking down the road. She looked lost, so I stopped and asked if I could help her.

"Turns out she'd gone hiking in Lorene Roberts the day before; she started in Aptos. She'd walked and walked and when night fell, she was lost. She kept walking, wandered around in there all night. Early in the morning she struck Rider Road, probably came out right through that apple orchard. She walked down Rider to Eureka Canyon, which was where I found her."

"So, are you suggesting that Barbara could be lost in the park? For three days?"

"I don't know," I said. "I just don't know. Lost on purpose, maybe. Two sets of hoofprints could mean she was leading a pack animal. Maybe she's living in the park, sort of like Mountain Dave, with horses instead of a bike."

Blue considered this awhile. "Why?" he asked.

"To get away. Rethink her life. It's something I could see myself doing."

Blue hugged me again. "After all, we met on a pack trip."

"That's right, we did." I stared straight ahead, feeling the comforting warmth of Blue's arm around my shoulders, seeing sunlight break through the clouds outside the window. But my mind was somewhere else. "I wish Mountain Dave would call," I said. "I want to know where those horses went."

Blue opened his mouth to say something else and the phone interrupted us once again. This time it was the answering service, with "a severely lame horse at Lee Castillo's place."

"Oh shit," I said, as I hung up the phone. "Another person with a reason to have killed Dominic calling me out."

"Let me go with you, Gail." Blue took my hand in his.

"It's really not necessary. Lee can hardly page me to come out to her place with an emergency and then shoot me. It's like signing her own death warrant. I'll be fine. And there's plenty to do around here."

"That's true enough, and I do need to go by work today and check on some plants." Blue squeezed my hand. "But I'll keep my cell phone with me. Call me if anything looks odd."

"I will. I promise."

And back into the truck I went.

TWENTY

Lee Castillo's place, when I reached it, looked deserted. A brisk wind had blown the rain clouds away, and sunlight spattered the old barn and farmhouse. Chickens pecked in the manure pile, horses grazed in the pasture, but no humans were in sight.

Here we go again, I thought. Despite my confident words to Blue, I was nervous. The encounter with Carlos Castillo had shaken me right down to my core. Clutching my cell phone in my hand, I climbed slowly out of the truck.

"Lee?" I called tentatively.

No answer.

At a guess, she was in the barn. Straightening my spine, I walked in that direction. "Lee?"

Still no answer. After a moment, I stepped inside the doorway.

It was an old building, perhaps of the same vintage as the barn on Elkhorn Slough, where Blue and I had camped. Like most barns of that era, the central space was open and high-roofed, meant to store hay. Lee's barn, I saw, housed a hefty stack of alfalfa. A row of box stalls ran down the two facing walls.

Horses peered out at me over the lower halves of their stall doors. Arabian faces—elegant, chiseled, black and gray and bay.

"Lee!" I called again.

Nothing.

The horses watched me; pigeons cooed in the rafters. Somewhere outside, I heard the plaintive descending call of a mourning dove.

For a long second I stared. The interior of the barn was dim and shadowy; barely perceived motion in the depths resolved itself into a black cat, leaping down from the haystack. I turned away.

Back outside, I took a deep breath of the clean air. The little spring rain was gone as if it had never been. A bright, sunny breeze tossed the eucalyptus trees behind the barn.

Lee must be in the house, I decided. Clients did sometimes wait by the phone, veterinarians being prone to calling in a warning of lateness. Resolutely, I marched toward the back porch.

The house was as old as the barn. The sagging wooden steps creaked and complained at my footfalls. I rapped on the doorframe as loudly as I could; the door itself stood ajar.

"Lee!" I shouted.

No response. The open door led to what was plainly the kitchen, which was obviously empty.

"Lee!" I yelled.

Nothing. Hesitantly, I stepped into the room. What could possibly have happened to Lee?

I crossed the kitchen and stuck my head through the open doorway on the far side. The living room, apparently. Couch, two armchairs by a fireplace, a piano. No people.

Holding my breath, I listened. I could hear the old house murmur, the tiniest of creaks and groans, a soft subtext to the silence. As in a redwood grove, the quiet felt palpable, even personal, as though somewhere there were eyes, watching me. I shivered, and turned to go.

"Jesus!" I yelped. There he stood in the doorway, eyes watching me intently. Dom.

I grabbed the back of the couch to steady myself, felt the great thumping *whoosh* as my heart took off in overdrive. Desperately I searched this hulking teenager's face for his intent.

I couldn't tell much. Dom's face was expressionless, the remains of his pudgy adolescence visible in the heavy, pasty features, puffy cheeks, sagging jawline. But the overall impression was of a meaty muscularity, a dormant power coiled sullenly in a torpid shell.

"Where's Lee?" I got the words out, finally.

"Mom's gone."

The tone was flat, but at least he'd replied in a relatively normal way to my question. There was no gun in his hand. Maybe my run-in with Carlos had made me overly nervy. Dom was just, I reassured myself, a normally sulky young male.

"I was called out here to see a lame horse," I said.

"I called you."

"All right. Can we see the horse? I couldn't find anyone out at the barn."

"I was out back. Working." Dom's impassive face told me nothing. Those odd light brown eyes, so like his mother's, were as unreadable as two marbles. I had no idea what was going on inside his head.

"I'll show you the horse." Dom turned and left the room.

I followed him with an audible sigh of relief. Perhaps there was nothing strange happening here after all. Just a lame horse and a morose teen.

Dom led me steadily towards the barn without a backward look; I trailed in his wake, trying to gather my professional composure back together. A lame horse. I was here to deal with a lame horse.

A very lame horse, it turned out. Dom brought a hobbling chestnut mare out of her box stall and said, "She was like this when I went out to the pasture to check the water. I brought her in and called your office."

138

I studied the mare, who was standing with just the toe of her right front hoof resting on the ground. Her leg didn't appear to be swollen anywhere. Don't forget the obvious, Gail, I reminded myself.

Stepping up to the horse, I ran a hand down her right foreleg and lifted the foot up. Using the hoofpick tool on the pocketknife I always carried, I cleaned the dirt out of the hoof. Bingo.

"She stepped on a nail," I told Dom. "See the nail head."

Dom peered where I pointed and said nothing.

"I'll pull it out, open up the puncture so it will drain, and wrap her foot. You'll need to give her antibiotics night and morning for ten days and rewrap the foot every other day."

"All right."

Getting the things I needed out of my truck, I returned to the mare and got started. Dom watched me work in unnerving silence. I had the idea there was something going on beneath that apparently wooden demeanor, but I still couldn't figure out what.

When the words came, they were completely unexpected. "They don't suspect Mom, do they?"

Involved as I was in my work, it took me a moment to process this. "You mean is she a suspect in Dominic's—your father's—murder?"

Dom nodded, the merest affirmative jerk of his chin.

I packed gauze soaked with weak iodine into the mare's hoof and said, "I'm really not the one to ask."

"That detective keeps questioning her. He says she called Dad's girlfriend that morning to find out where Dad was going to be. I never thought . . ." The words tumbled out and trickled to a stop.

"You never thought what?" I wrapped the mare's foot with elasticized gauze and began on a layer of duct tape.

"That Mom would be suspected."

For a second I glimpsed what I thought was mute misery beneath the stoic exterior, and then all was frozen again. Dom met my stare, his own glance impervious.

"Lots of us were or are suspects," I said, as I smoothed the last strip of duct tape in place.

"Besides Mom?"

This time I was sure of the briefly revealed emotion on Dom's face. Pure, unadulterated relief. Banished almost as soon as it appeared; nonetheless, it was there.

Handing him antibiotics and instructions, I said, "Yes, besides your mom."

After another minute to make sure Dom knew what to do to take care of the mare, I turned away and made my escape, my mind churning. What was going on here?

I climbed into my truck with certain phrases bouncing around in my head like pinballs. A young man had called Barbara that day, asking Dominic's whereabouts. Who else would Dominic want to shield more than his own son? Had Dom known that his father was leaving him money? And, "I never thought they'd suspect Mom." Dom's words. Had he imagined he could kill his father without Lee coming under investigation?

I bounced down yet another rutted driveway full of potholes with my mind in as high a gear as the truck was in low. Too much information—I couldn't seem to organize it in any useful way.

Once again I pointed the truck for home, and Blue, seeking advice and comfort, not necessarily in that order.

TWENTY-ONE

W hen I got home, Blue was gone. There was a note on the table in his neat printing.

I'm at work. Call me if you need me. Mountain Dave called.
The two horses came out of the park at Summit Road. Dave
hasn't talked to the cyclist named John yet, but he says he'll
keep looking. And Dave absolutely will not talk to the police.

Love to you—Blue

Slowly I set the piece of paper down on the table. The horses, and possibly Barbara, had exited Lorene Roberts at Summit Road. I knew exactly where—a dirt road I'd hiked down myself, many years ago. What if . . . if?

What was it Barbara had said? She had a sister named Paula who lived on Summit Road. What if Barbara had merely chosen an unconventional way to go stay with her sister? And how in the world could I find her, armed simply with the knowledge of a woman named Paula who lived on Summit Road.

I tried getting a Paula King's phone number out of the information operator. No luck.

What now? Drumming my fingers on the table, I stared out the big windows into the garden.

Midafternoon was easing into the mellow, golden light of late afternoon. Some pale pink sweet peas that twined along the vegetable garden fence shone incandescently in a long fall of sunlight. Without thinking, I stood up and walked out the door. Onto the porch, where pots of purple pansies waited, and on down the steps and into the garden. I needed to think.

To think, and to be replenished by the plants and animals, by Nature, vivid and lively all around me. By the robin splashing in the birdbath and the rabbit nibbling rosebushes at the side of the path. By nasturtiums in a fountain of mandarin orange and cranesbill geraniums in mounding pillows of magenta purple. I paused to sniff one perfect blossom of the single rose called Summer Wine; the flower glowed an intense coral-pink with wine red stamens at the heart; it smelled otherworldly, of a pure and delicious sweetness.

Blue had put Roey in the dog pen; he must have taken Freckles with him. I let my little red dog out and watched her run through the long grass, ears back, mouth open in a happy grin.

Walking down to the barn, I greeted each of the horses in turn, rubbing necks, straightening forelocks, checking to see that water troughs were clean and full. I spent a little extra time with Mr. Twister, admiring his shadowed silver and charcoal hair coat, stroking his shoulder, making sure that he looked reasonably comfortable.

And then I sat down on a hay bale and stared straight ahead of me. The big eucalyptus tree on the ridge raised its shaggy branches high in the spring sunshine. Oaks in the foreground dappled the grass with flickering shadows. Black Jiji Cat slid out from behind the barn and lay down on the loose chaff next to me—more or less on the spot where Dominic had fallen.

Time passed. The horses strolled about their corrals, relaxed and content, the spring breeze playing with their manes and tails. Slanted shafts of sunlight angled into the barn as the sun dipped towards the western ridge. I could smell the faint, heady sweetness of blooming ceanothus in the air. I sat and I stared and I thought. Some time later, I knew what to do.

Evening was drawing in as I fed each of the horses a flake of hay. I fed the cats and the chickens; I shut Roey back in her pen and fed her, too. Leaving Blue a quick note: "Went up to Summit Road to find Barbara King's sister, Paula," I climbed into my pickup and headed out.

I went the long way, took my time. So many thoughts were rambling around inside my head; I was having a hard time keeping track of them. But the one that kept arising most persistently was a simple question. Was Barbara dead or alive? Somehow I felt that once I knew the answer, things would fall into place.

The sun sank slowly over the Monterey Bay; I could see a sunset in my rearview mirror as I drove up Eureka Canyon Road. Banners of apricot drifted out across the sky. I reached a wide spot in the road and pulled over.

Hills and ridges spread out below me, rumpled as a tossed velvet skirt. Silhouetted pines and redwoods darkened from misty blue to ash as orange-red streaks intensified across the sky. A thin band glowed peacock green on the horizon; the distant bay was a cold, remote gray-blue.

Rolling down the window of my truck, I breathed in the aromatic redwood/sagebrush scent, herbal and clean. The hills before me, I realized, were part of Lorene Roberts Park. What was the story? I'd heard it somewhere: the park had once belonged to the Roberts family—a vast tract of land, it was far too steep and wooded to be called a ranch. It had been logged several times, until Lorene had inherited it and donated the land to the state. From this vista, the hills looked endlessly wild, untouched by man, an ideal place to get lost.

The thought brought Barbara back to the front of my mind. Was her body out there, lying in some ravine? I started the truck and drove on.

On towards the ridgeline and Summit Road. Eureka Canyon Road was getting narrower and rougher by the minute. I hadn't been this way in several years, and it looked as though there had been a few landslides since then. At times I was reduced to a one-lane dirt track skirting some outsize pile of loose rubble.

Dusk was turning to dark; the prospect of being stuck out here was not inviting. Houses were few and far between, and I began to wish I had taken the more conventional route.

Too late to turn back now. By my reckoning, I ought to strike Summit Road pretty damn soon.

The truck jolted me up and down; oak trees leaned at crazy angles over what remained of the road. I began to long for a vestige of human civilization, even another pair of headlights in the gloom.

No such appeared. As far as I could tell, I was driving through the wilderness, all alone. A person really could get lost out here, I reflected.

Miles and miles of empty mountainous forest rolled away around me; not a sign of a human dwelling visible for as far as I could see. I rounded another hairpin turn with some caution, and sighed in relief as my headlights showed me the narrow paved strip of Summit Road. Thank God.

I turned left, towards houses and people, and reminded myself of the reason for my trip. I was here to find Barbara, if I could. And I had a plan.

I drove, eventually passing the occasional light of a solitary house. Not too far now. In another five miles, more or less, I turned in to a narrow driveway and piloted the truck up to a quiet barn. I'd arrived.

TWENTY-TWO

I got out of my pickup and peered around. The house was dark, but there were lights on at the barn. Hopefully, I walked in that direction.

Stepping through the open doorway, I paced down a long row of stalls, automatically peering at the horses inside. Here a sorrel with a flaxen mane and tail, next a buckskin, next a bay. Everybody's head was down, munching on hay. I could hear the familiar rustle and chomp of horses eating, could smell the sweetness of alfalfa hay and pine shavings mingling with the rich, warm scent of the horses themselves.

Slowly I coasted to a standstill, almost forgetting my purpose. There was nothing like a barn for feeling peaceful, I reflected. Barns were every bit as harmonious as gardens.

Lost in my thoughts, I stared blankly at the horse in front of me without really seeing him. It took a moment, but recognition finally dawned. I knew this horse.

A black-and-white paint gelding, he had a distinctive off-center blaze. For a long second I stared; the horse continued to eat, undisturbed by my presence. I was sure. This was Barbara's horse.

145

Glancing wildly up and down the barn aisle, I looked for some sign of a human presence, uncertain now whether I hoped or feared to be greeted. What could it possibly mean that Barbara's horse was in this barn?

My mind roved frantically through the possibilities; none of them were good. Turning, I headed back down the barn aisle at a good brisk clip. I wanted out of here. I would think about what this meant when I was safely back home.

I'd gone maybe a dozen steps when the lights went out. A tiny, whispered click, and sudden darkness. I froze, every sense on the alert.

As my eyes adjusted, I was aware of a grayish square of light somewhere ahead of me—the doorway. All else was black.

Was this an accident? Had someone turned off the barn lights, not knowing I was there? Or? I didn't like to consider the other options.

The most natural thing would have been to call out, "Hello," but somehow I didn't want to do that. I stayed frozen in place, making no sound, breathing as quietly as I could, and waited for some clue as to what was happening.

Even as I hesitated, I took inventory. I had nothing useful. No gun, no cell phone, no flashlight. No matches, even. I had nothing that even remotely resembled a weapon, unless you could count a pocketknife.

The cell phone, and a flashlight, were out in my truck, which suddenly seemed as if it were light-years away. I waited.

I could hear the steady munching of the horses, the rustle of hay and shavings underfoot. Somewhere in the distance an owl hooted. That was it. I held my breath.

Slowly the blackness grew less absolute as my eyes adjusted themselves. The stalls, I realized, had doors to the outside, and the top halves of these doors were open. Some gentle silver-white moonlight filtered in.

Turning my head, I stared into the stall next to me. There was the dark shape of the horse, head down, eating. Behind him was a square of night sky. The way out, if I could get there.

I took a step towards the stall, then stopped to listen. Nothing. Another step. Nothing. Then another and another. I put my hand on the stall door latch and started to slide the bolt back.

Even as the metal bolt rasped against the latch, I heard the click. Heard it and saw it at once, as a piercing flood of brilliant light blinded me. Blinking, I brought my hand up to shield my eyes from the flashlight beam and heard the voice.

"Don't move."

The tone was harsh, but I recognized the human being behind it.

"Oh," I said. "How are you, Sandy?"

TWENTY-THREE

W hat the hell are you doing sneaking around my barn? I thought you were a burglar." Sandy McQuire sounded righteously pissed off.

For a moment that seemed to take hours, my brain stumbled, searching for a possible answer to this question. It had seemed plausible enough at the time to drive up here and ask Sandy if she knew where Barbara's sister lived. Not now. Right now, the last thing in the world I wanted to mention was Barbara King's name.

Sandy would not, I realized a split second later, know that I'd seen and recognized Barbara's horse. I just needed to come up with a reasonable excuse for being here.

"I'm sorry, Sandy" was what came out of my mouth. "I was in the area and wondered how that bay horse was doing. The one with the intermittent colics. I thought I'd check on him. I didn't see any lights on in the house, so I was looking for you out at the barn." The last part of this was true, anyway.

Sandy was still regarding me with a suspicious eye.

I tried a friendly smile. "So, how is the horse doing?"

"Leo? You're looking at him."

I blinked and focused my gaze on the animal in the stall in front of me. Dark bay, unremarkable, head down eating, like the rest of them.

"Is that him?" I asked.

"That's him," Sandy said. Her tone was not cordial.

"He looks like he's doing well. Any more colicky spells?" I knew I was driveling on; I guessed that Sandy wasn't buying the ostensible reason for my presence. But she stood between me and that open doorway at the end of the barn aisle—the doorway that led to my truck and freedom. Somehow I needed to allay her suspicions.

"He's been all right." Sandy was curt. Then, "Why don't you have a look at him?"

"All right." Opening the stall door, I stepped inside. Leo looked up from his hay, assessed me briefly, and went back to eating. I saw a halter hanging on a hook near his water bucket and stepped towards it.

Crash! I spun to see the stall door slammed shut; I could hear the bolts shooting home in the latches. Even as I took this in, a corresponding crash on the other side of the stall caused both Leo and me to jump. Someone had shut the top half of the Dutch door that opened to the outside. The click of the closing latch was plainly audible.

I was, I realized, trapped in this stall with Leo. A second later, the faint light leaking under the door disappeared; I could hear Sandy walking away.

Black, black dark. No light of any sort. I raised my hand to touch my face—couldn't see my fingers even when I could feel them.

My God. My heart thumped crazily inside my chest; my mind spun. Sandy had locked me in this stall. Not just Sandy—two people, one at each door. Barbara's horse was in Sandy's barn. This did not add up to a good outcome. What in the hell could I do?

Even as my mind dithered, I assessed the possibilities. I couldn't see at all. The stall wasn't big, maybe twelve feet by twelve feet. Leo was in it; I could hear him munching next to me, apparently not bothered by my incarceration in his home. What had Sandy said, that Leo was "gentle as a pup"?

What else was in the stall? A five-gallon plastic water bucket and a halter on a peg. In the corner closest to me.

I took a deep breath, tried to quiet my racing heart. Unless I missed my guess, I needed to consider some evasive action. Sandy was not going to leave me locked in her box stall indefinitely. And I had an idea what the alternative might be.

Darkness was absolute, omnipresent, palpable. It was more than the absence of light; it felt like a viscous, inky substance, a weight bearing down. Fanciful as it seemed, blackness was oppressively frightening.

I blinked my eyes. Nothing changed. Only blackness.

I touched my nose again and felt a rush of pure terror as I realized I couldn't see my own fingers, though they were maybe an inch from my eyes. It was almost as if I'd disappeared.

Calm down. Calm down. It's just dark. I tried to soothe myself by focusing on the sound of Leo's rhythmic *chomp, chomp, chomp*. And in that instant, I knew what to do.

Without hesitation I inched my way forward, feeling with my hands until I touched the stall wall. Guiding myself by touch only, I worked my way along the wall until I came to the corner. Sure enough, there was the halter on its peg. My feet found the round solidness of the plastic bucket full of water.

Slowly, gently, I tipped the bucket over, guiding it so that the water ran away from me. I took the halter and leadrope down from the peg.

With halter in one hand and bucket in the other, I inched my way across the stall towards the munching Leo. This was the difficult part. I prayed that Leo was, in truth, as gentle as a pup.

Reaching out with the hand that held the halter, I felt for the horse, knowing he was nearby, not knowing exactly which part of his anatomy I might touch. After a minute, I found the smooth, sleek warmth of his hair coat.

I stroked him awhile, decided that what I was feeling was his rib cage. Working my way in what I hoped was the right direction, I came to the rough, stringy texture of his mane. Good.

I was on Leo's left side, in the appropriate position. All I had to do was put his halter on by feel.

Easier said than done. I felt down Leo's neck, and pushed on him gently to raise his head from his meal. The head came up; I could tell by the position of his neck and the cessation of chomping sounds. Leo snorted softly.

Reaching out, I felt around in the blackness, trying to pull what I thought was the noseband of the halter over the horse's nose.

Leo helped me. Like many gentle, cooperative horses will do, he stuck his face in the halter.

"How the hell did you see that?" I whispered as I fumbled around his ears to buckle the halter strap.

Horses have much better night vision than humans—I knew this—but I couldn't imagine that any creature would see anything in this impenetrable gloom.

No time for that. Leo was caught. I felt with my foot and hand until I located his flake of hay, then half dragged, half shoved it until it was in the corner of the stall. Then I turned the bucket upside down and placed it next to the wall, in what I thought was the right position.

Holding Leo's leadrope in one hand, I felt for his body with the other. Guiding him with the halter and my hand against his rib cage, I positioned him until his head was in the corner with his hay and his body was lined up along the stall wall.

Carefully I squeezed under his neck and crept along the wall until I felt the bucket with my foot. Leo dropped his head and went back to eating hay, seeming quite content to stand there.

Using his body to steady myself, I climbed up on the bucket. Then I crouched down, my back against the stall wall, my nose pressed to Leo's rib cage, the leadrope in my left hand. Not exactly the most comfortable position, but one that I could maintain for a little while if I tried.

With any luck at all, I wouldn't have to wait too long. Surely, I thought, the move to dispose of me would come sooner, rather than later. Much safer, especially if I'd told anyone where I was going.

Which I hadn't, like an idiot. I'd told Blue that I'd gone to find Barbara's sister, Paula; I hadn't mentioned that I'd planned to ask Sandy McQuire where Paula lived. I took another deep breath and concentrated on holding my position. Prayed that Leo would hold still. Prayed fervently that I was right—that a person looking in this stall wouldn't see me, that my body was hidden behind Leo's barrel, my feet up on the bucket, my head down below his withers. At first glance, anyway, the stall would appear empty except for the horse.

A moment—that was all I was going to get, if I was lucky. A moment and an open door. I prayed.

My back ached, my legs ached. I tried to relax my muscles, relax my body. I asked that the moment of truth come quickly, before I stiffened too much. I thanked God that Leo seemed quite willing to stand quietly, parallel to the stall wall, eating his hay.

And then I heard it. The softest of noises, but unmistakable to one who was listening for just that sound. Footfalls in the barn aisle. Someone was coming.

The footsteps came to a halt outside my stall, just as I had known they would. I took another breath and asked for the strength to do what I needed to do.

I heard a click, a very gentle, singular click. The sound of the bolt, one bolt, being drawn back. At a guess, the top half of the Dutch door.

The lights stayed off; the blackness remained impenetrable. But I knew that someone was peering into the stall over the bottom half of the door. I waited.

The moment, when it came, was too fast for thought. I heard the click as the flashlight beam blazed in, heard another click that I knew in my gut was a single-action pistol being cocked. I gathered myself.

For a second the flashlight roamed the stall; I heard the muttered "What the hell?"

Not the voice I'd expected. My God. Once again my mind reeled in shock, trying to process the new information.

Then there was the sound of another bolt sliding back. My eyes, adjusting rapidly, saw the figure step into the stall. The door was open.

Light swept around the walls—only a moment remained before I was inevitably discovered.

In that moment, I leaped onto Leo's back from the bucket, pulling myself up with the hand that was twined in his mane. Even as the figure whirled with a startled shout, I kicked Leo forward, guiding him with the leadrope. Right at the human being in the middle of the stall.

I heard a yell, saw the person lurch away, and drummed my heels into Leo's sides, urging him toward the open stall doorway. He lunged for the gap just as the stall seemed to explode with sound.

Gunshot. I crouched low over Leo's neck, tucked my knees and feet into his sides and hung on for all I was worth as he crashed through the doorway.

Then we were charging down the barn aisle, as another shot rang out behind us.

Leo panicked; he was running headlong, out of control, my tugs on the leadrope had no effect. I wrapped both hands in his mane and clung like a burr with feet and knees and thighs.

I had no idea where Leo was taking me as we sailed out of the barn and into the night, but it didn't really matter. Anywhere was better than here.

TWENTY-FOUR

The moon was up, hard and almost full and white; I could see shapes in its light as we crashed across the stable yard in a flurry of pounding hooves. Like the creature of habit that a horse is, Leo appeared to be making straight for a little riding ring that I could see ahead of us—no doubt the place he was exercised every day.

Good. I could probably regain control of him there. I encouraged his tendency with my hands on the leadrope and we galloped through the open gate of the arena.

Once inside, I worked at pulling Leo's head around to the left, tugging on the leadrope with one hand while I clung to his mane with the other. I gave eternal thanks that he had a flat back and smooth gaits; were it not for that, I was certain I'd be lying on the ground.

"Come on, Leo," I said out loud.

The horse yielded to my tugs, circling to a stop in the center of the ring. I took a deep breath and looked back the way we'd come.

Oh, shit.

A figure stood at the gate to the arena, silhouetted in the moonlight. I could see the pistol, not pointed at me, not yet, but there in the right hand.

And I could hear the voice, a little out of breath, but sounding quite calm and in charge.

"You can stop running now, Gail. There isn't anywhere to go."

I glanced wildly around, but could see no other open gates. Taking another breath, I tried to steady myself.

"So," I said, "you're alive, Barbara."

"Surely you knew that by now."

"I just figured it out five minutes ago, when you stuck your head in that stall with every intention of shooting me."

"Well, you are slow." Barbara laughed. "I was sure you'd recognize old Paint. When Sandy told me who was in the barn, I knew it was time to take care of you."

"I did recognize your horse," I admitted. "But I'm afraid I thought that Sandy must have killed you."

"Sandy didn't kill anyone." I could hear Barbara's smile, though I couldn't see it. "I did."

"You killed Dominic?" I was honestly shocked. Leo shifted restlessly, and I reached down to touch his neck with my free hand.

"That's right, I killed the bastard."

"But . . ." I still couldn't quite take it in, "You seemed so devastated. I believed you."

"Gail, you're not as smart as I thought you were. I loved Dominic. I miss him like my right arm. But I'd rather he was dead than living with that blond bitch."

"Tracy?"

"That's right. Dear little Tracy."

"You killed Tracy, too," I said slowly.

"Right again. Why should she go on having a happy life after she ruined mine?"

I touched Leo's neck with my hand, feeling the warm, soft hair. It was grounding, a steady island in the rising tide of disillusionment swelling over me. Alone in the moonlit arena, facing the prospect of my own imminent demise, I acknowledged the truth. Barbara had loved Dominic—enough to kill him. Enough to kill the woman he had chosen over her. It might not be a kind of love I understood, but history books and classical tragedies were full of its like.

"So Dominic told you he was leaving you for Tracy on Friday, the same day Tracy told Sam."

"Did she?" Barbara sounded quite indifferent. "They must have had a little agreement." Her voice rose suddenly, a strident squawk. "For all the good it did them. That bastard Dominic just told me flat he was leaving me for her. No ifs, ands, or buts. I begged, I pleaded, I cried; he acted like he didn't give a flying fuck. Then I told him I'd stop him, whatever it took. He laughed." Barbara paused for breath. "He isn't laughing now," she said flatly.

"Why me?" I asked her. "Why did you kill him at my place? Why drag me into it? I had nothing to do with Dominic."

Barbara snorted. "You're such a goody two-shoes, Gail. Dominic used to talk about you all the time, every time he'd shoe your horse. How pretty you were, how smart you were, how much he'd like to go out with you. I hated it."

"Barbara," I said, I hoped calmly, "Dominic flirted with everyone. You must have known that."

"Of course I knew that. But you were just so perfect. A horse vet and all. You make me sick. When I decided to kill Dominic, I checked his schedule. As soon as I saw your name as his last call of the day, I knew that's where I would do it. I even passed you on the road as I was leaving; I worried you'd seen me."

"Well, I didn't," I said honestly. "Did you make up all those phone calls—people asking where Dominic was?"

"Only one of them." Barbara snorted. "Lee and Sam did call, just as described."

"And you, instead of riding in Lorene Roberts, you drove over to my place, took Dominic's gun out of his glove compartment, and shot him."

"That's right. You should thank me. I made him move away from your horse first, in case I missed."

"So, that's why Dominic lied," I said slowly. "He was protecting you."

For the first time Barbara's voice faltered. "That was the worst thing. To know he took care of me, even after I killed him. He must have known that I loved him too much to live without him. I guess he forgave me."

I said nothing. Leo shifted under me, and I let my eyes drift around the riding ring.

"And then you killed Tracy," I said. "Did you cut the palomino horse's throat just to get me out there?"

"Now that's clever of you, Gail," Barbara said. "That's more than I expected from you. You're right, I did cut that horse so that the blond bitch would call you out. I parked my truck behind some old horse trailers and just waited around for my opportunity. Those stupid people had no idea I was there. I nipped in a stall after Sam left for town, slashed the horse, and went back to my truck and waited some more. I shot that miserable Tracy as soon as you left; I thought you'd make an ideal suspect."

"And did you tell Sandy to call me out right afterward?"

"That's very good," Barbara said in an admiring tone. "I did. I wanted to keep you in the area awhile, make it look as if you would have had plenty of time to kill Tracy and hide the gun in Sam's tack room. I told Sandy to tell you Leo, there, was colicked."

"So, what's Sandy have to do with this?"

"Sandy and I have been friends a long time," Barbara said. "Dominic screwed her over years ago. She warned me not to get involved with him. I should have listened, but I didn't. I didn't tell her I killed him; she guessed."

"And offered to help you out," I hazarded.

"Right again. That fucking detective was just determined to suspect me. I thought if I disappeared for a while, he might think someone had killed me, too."

"So you called Sam Lawrence up and talked him into coming over to your place on Thursday morning."

"Told him I had a nice horse to sell him, real cheap. He was there an hour later. I sold him the horse and he hauled it away. I just hope to hell some of the neighbors saw him."

"They did." I stroked Leo's neck and contemplated the far corner of the riding ring.

"Good," Barbara said. "Hopefully that bastard Sam is arrested by now."

"And you just took off with a saddle horse and a pack horse and rode through Lorene Roberts Park and up here to Sandy's. Nobody saw you but some guy on a mountain bike."

"Now I am impressed." Barbara whistled. "How'd you work that out?"

"We tracked you," I said. "I had this feeling you might have ridden into the park, though to begin with I thought it might have been to kill yourself."

"I thought of it. But I decided not to give up so easily. I'll stay here at Sandy's awhile. And when I reappear, I will just have taken some time to be alone and grieve. By then Sam Lawrence ought to have a trial date."

"What about me?" I said quietly.

"Surely you know what I plan to do about you." Barbara's voice was as quiet as my own. "Do you think I'm likely to let you steal my horse and ride on out of here?"

"How about borrow him? Heck, I'll settle for my truck. You let me get in and drive away, and I won't say a word about anything you've told me."

"No chance. I don't trust you."

"It won't work to kill me. I told my boyfriend where I was going. Cops will be all over this place if I don't get home within the hour." How I wished this were true.

Barbara sighed. "I'm betting against it. I don't think you told anyone, Gail. I think you're bluffing, and I'm going to call your bluff. This is where it ends, here and now."

At the chill in her words, my heart accelerated. I could feel my leg muscles tighten against Leo's sides. In response, the horse danced, tossing his head.

I calculated the distance. Barbara held a pistol; from a hundred feet away she was unlikely to be terribly accurate. At least, this was what I was betting. And she wasn't likely to expect my next move.

I'd had plenty of time to study my options; I was ready. As Barbara raised the pistol, I pointed Leo's head toward the far corner of the ring and drummed my heels against his sides.

The horse launched himself like a rocket off its pad. I clung to him with feet and hands, ducked low over his neck, as the shot rang out.

I didn't know if we were hit; I had no time or space for anything but riding. Riding and urging the galloping Leo towards that low spot in the fence. I could see that the top rail was broken. The remaining two rails were only three feet high. Any horse can jump three feet.

Can, but won't, maybe. I didn't care. If Leo wouldn't jump this fence, I was going to drive him right through it. It looked as though some horse had broken the top rail; we could break the bottom two.

Another shot rang out, and another. Barbara could see my intent now. But the shots worked in my favor.

I could feel Leo hesitate as he approached the fence, but the loud explosions behind him catapulted him forward. He accelerated, gathered himself; I knew he would jump.

I had no idea if I could stay on. I had never tried to jump a horse bareback in my life.

Now, now, now. I urged with hands and feet; I gripped Leo's mane and put my weight forward, over his shoulders and neck.

Leo jumped. A huge jump—he cleared what was left of the fence cleanly, as yet another shot crashed out behind us. He stumbled on landing, and I thought I was gone, but somehow I managed to stay on, clinging like a burr through sheer willpower.

Even as the horse picked himself up, he charged, completely out of my control. He clattered across the road behind the arena—Summit Road, I realized—and took off down a trail that twisted between redwood trees. He seemed sure of himself, as if he knew the way. Since I couldn't stop him anyway, I devoted all my attention to staying on.

Branches whipped my face; stripes of moonlight and shadow barred the trail in black and white. I tried to stay balanced and in the middle of Leo, tried to keep my head down just above his neck.

In a minute, I knew where we were going. This trail ran alongside Summit Road. Not too far from here it would strike an old logging road that I was familiar with. Leo was probably taking the route that Sandy used when she went out for a trail ride. Leo was taking me right into the heart of Lorene Roberts Park.

TWENTY-FIVE

There was little I could do about it. Barbara and her gun were behind me; I could hardly turn around and go back. Having revealed herself so completely, Barbara desperately needed to kill me. I hung on to Leo as well as I could and rode on.

Trees surrounded me; brush formed a wall on both sides of the trail. Moonlight shafted through gaps, but I could see little. All my energy went into clinging to Leo's back and avoiding the branches that swiped at me.

To my great relief, I could feel the horse beginning to tire. His gait shifted from a headlong run to a more manageable gallop; I could feel his heart thumping. My jeans were growing damp from his sweat. I gave a few tentative tugs on the leadrope, and Leo coasted to a stop in a little clearing, both of us breathing hard.

Our trail had joined up with the logging road that I remembered. I could see the dirt road, open and silvery in the moonlight, running up the hill ahead of me. If I followed it long enough, I knew, I would eventually reach the bridge where Blue and I had run into Mountain

Dave. And on beyond that lay the cutoff trail to Rider Road and the other side of the park. If I had to, I could ride home.

This was not an idea I was enamored of. Nonetheless, I liked it a lot better than going back. Barbara was back there somewhere with her gun, and I wanted no part of that.

I would survive, I thought, if I rode through the park. I was wearing only jeans and a denim shirt, but the mild spring night wasn't particularly chilly, and Leo's back was warm. Riding him bareback for fifteen miles would probably make me so sore I'd be in bed for a week, but anything was better than facing that gun.

Leo shifted restlessly under me, and I reached down to pat his neck. The road awaited us, looking invitingly wide and clear compared to the trail we had just navigated. We could do it; Leo seemed fit and bold and sure-footed enough. I'd be home by morning.

Taking a deep breath of resolution, I started to urge the horse forward. His body froze, his head came up, and he looked back the way we'd come. He nickered.

I looked where he was looking, and my heart shifted back into high gear with a lurch. A horse, galloping down the trail in our wake. A black-and-white paint with a rider. Barbara.

Once again I thumped my heels hard into Leo's sides and he leaped forward. Up the road, up the hill, into the park. I had no useful ideas, no plans; I just ran for my life.

One glance had told me that Barbara was riding her paint horse bareback, just as I was riding Leo. Moonlight glinted on the chunk of metal in her hand. Barbara was desperate to catch me and kill me; it was her only chance at survival.

The logging road was relatively open, the slope not too steep. Our brief rest had given Leo a chance to catch his air; he was running gamely. Another glance over my shoulder showed that Barbara wasn't gaining.

Sandy McQuire had said that Leo was talented and athletic; I hoped to hell that he was fast, too. It would be, I thought, impossible for Barbara to shoot me with a pistol from the back of a galloping horse at any distance at all. She would have to catch me first, and that, I thought, I could prevent.

Leo galloped up the road confidently enough, seeming sure of his footing. I imagined that Sandy probably rode him this way often, and he knew the terrain. I hoped so, anyway. I prayed that the road would continue to run uphill for a good long way. I wasn't sure I'd be able to stay on Leo going downhill at a gallop.

Even as I rode, my mind raced, taking in the significance of Barbara's pursuit. She must have run straight back to the barn when I'd jumped out of the riding ring, caught her paint horse, climbed on him, and ridden after me. It was the action of a truly desperate woman, a woman, I realized a split second later, who had nothing left to lose. Barbara would pursue me until either she or I was dead.

Assimilating this thought, I urged Leo to go faster. Redwoods were a blurry skyscape far above me, the dirt road gray-white in the moon's cold glow. This eerie world was a nightmare; I wanted to wake up.

Help me, please. I prayed the words, not knowing exactly who I was praying to. That which is, which animates the moonlit world. In another second, to the pounding of Leo's hooves and the grunt of his breath, the answer came.

Barbara would have just as much difficulty riding her horse bareback as I was having. Like me, she was used to riding in a saddle. Desperation had caused her to take this chance, but it could work in my favor.

I could feel my leg muscles tiring, could feel Leo tiring underneath me as well. The road rose over a little hump and started down a steep hill. Looking over my shoulder, I could see that Barbara had lost ground, and the paint horse was merely loping. Leo had outrun him.

164

Tugging on the leadrope, I slowed my mount to a jog. He was happy to oblige; I could feel his breath coming in great heaving gasps.

The road descended abruptly and steeply, switchbacking through trees. Somewhere far below, I could hear water running over rocks. Moonlight showed me a steep canyon; our road clung to one bank.

I jogged around another blind corner and made up my mind. Now was better than later; both Leo and I were tiring fast.

Pulling hard with the leadrope and kicking with my outside leg, I forced Leo into the lee side of a big boulder that anchored the switchback. In this spot, we would be hidden from the oncoming horse.

My denim was innocuous; Leo was a solid dark bay. Nothing white to catch the eye. Stroking Leo's neck, I implored him to hold perfectly still.

Fortunately, staying still sounded good to Leo. He was tired. He put his head down and sucked in air, more than ready to take a rest.

I could hear the quick *clip-chop* of shod hooves approaching, the horse going at a brisk jog. I smoothed Leo's mane, talked to him silently with my mind. Hold still, hold still, don't nicker.

Leo stayed quiet. My heart accelerated with adrenaline and fear. In another second, I could see the white patch on the paint horse's neck, shining in the moonlight, Barbara's face silhouetted over his neck. Then they were hidden by the big rock.

One more second. I gathered myself, tightened the leadrope, squeezed with my legs. Even as the paint horse's head came around the rock, I acted.

Slamming my legs into Leo as hard as I could, I jumped him forward, yelling at the top of my lungs, my free hand waving wildly in the air.

I caught the barest glimpse of Barbara's shocked face as her horse leaped sideways in a startled spook. The paint slipped on the edge of the bank; I thought he would go over, but he caught himself and scrambled back up on the trail. Not Barbara.

Flung hard to the outside by the momentum of the horse's leap, she lost her tenuous grip on her mount. I heard her yell, saw her body falling—off the horse, off the side of the bank, and down, down into the canyon.

Leo and I both jumped as the pistol went off with a violent boom that echoed and shuddered from the canyon walls. Slowly the sound died away. Leo and the paint horse stood nose to nose, both still puffing. Other than their breathing and the distant chatter of the creek, there was silence. Barbara was gone.

TWENTY-SIX

What seemed like a long, long time later, I gathered myself to go on. On into the park, I decided. It was tempting to go back—so much shorter. And there in Sandy's backyard was my truck, with my cell phone on the dash.

But I thought better of it. Sandy had locked me in a box stall; Sandy probably knew that Barbara intended to kill me. Perhaps Sandy hadn't killed anyone yet, but it seemed to me that there might be an easy progression from cooperating with a murderer to becoming one. I had no intention of offering myself as her first victim.

Blue might be searching for me by now, but he would have no idea where to look. Summit Road ran for many miles along the ridgeline; even if Blue could locate Barbara's sister, I hadn't a hope in hell that she would just happen to live within hailing distance of Sandy.

However difficult it might seem, onward was the direction of help and safety. No one would pursue me now; I just had to keep riding down this road until I got to the other side of the park, where there was a ranger station.

I was well aware that I wasn't likely to reach that station until dawn, but I reassured myself that I could do it. I had survived Barbara; I could survive an all-night ride.

Gathering Paint's leadrope up in my free hand, I led him along with us. The two horses were clearly buddies, and I knew Paint would have followed Leo whether I led him or not. Best to keep the whole thing under control.

On we went. Down and down and down, until we reached the bottom of the canyon and started back up. As we topped the ridge, I forgot my aching legs and frozen fingers and toes.

High in the night sky, the almost full moon shone, illuminating a silver-and-black tapestry of rolling forested hills that tumbled down to the distant curve of the Monterey Bay. A shimmering trail of moonlight danced on the water; I could see the faraway lights of Santa Cruz to the north and Monterey to the south.

"Wow," I said softly.

The horses stood perfectly still, staring, as if they were admiring the view, too. Even the forest was still. I forgot Barbara; I forgot what had brought me to this place. I gazed at the moonlit world in awestruck silence and gave thanks that I was here to see it.

I don't know how long I stood there. I do know that eventually I rode on, in a mesmerized trance. For many long miles I gripped Leo's back as we trudged uphill and plodded down. Dark, tree-clad tunnels gave way to brief clearings over and over again.

At one point I lifted my head to see a buck deer step into the trail in front of me. Leo pricked his ears and snorted but didn't spook; he'd clearly seen deer before. Moonlight dappled the animal; I could discern the fuzzy shapes of his growing antlers, still covered in velvet. For a long second he stared into my eyes, then Paint stomped a foot and the buck leaped into the forest and vanished to the sound of breaking brush. I rode on, feeling oddly comforted.

Alone, adrift in this endless wilderness—or so it seemed to me now—I suddenly felt connected in small, magical ways to the animating life. Leo carried me patiently; the buck had appeared to me as a protective sign. I would be protected; I had already been protected, I realized. I had only to trust—in myself and in the constant illuminating spirit of all that is.

Familiar as the horses in my corrals at home, the roses on my garden fence, the intuitive voice was always there, and it would lead me where I needed to go.

This was true, of course. And this time it was leading me on a long, long ride. I ached all over. My hands and feet were numb; my legs were so tired they trembled. We climbed ridges and descended into canyons; the moon hung straight overhead. I stared at the off-center white stripe that glowed on Paint's black face as he walked next to my right knee.

This is more than I can do. The thought wandered into my brain. I can't go on. I need to stop. I need to get off this horse. I need to rest. I need help.

I rode. Even as my mind made plaintive protests, my body stubbornly clung to Leo, and Leo walked. On and on and on.

At one point, as we plodded through yet another endless tunnel of trees, I was startled by sudden yips and a high-pitched keening that sounded only feet away. Even as I tugged on Leo's leadrope with my free hand, more voices joined the chorus—a crescendo of yips and howls. Coyotes. Their singing echoed sweetly through the hills. Leo paused and lifted his head; Paint pricked his ears. We all listened. As abruptly as it had begun, the song died away with one long, mournful howl. I clucked to Leo with a sigh that was equally mournful. On we went.

I need to rest. The words chanted in my brain to the cadence of Leo's steady gait. I could think of nothing but my sore and weary body, desperate for an end to this grueling ride.

Once again we were descending into a canyon; running water clattered somewhere ahead. On and on, through the trees, down and down. I was impossibly tired; every part of my body ached.

Judging by the sound of the water, we were almost at the bottom. As the moon shone through a gap in the trees, I saw the sparkling, moving light of the creek, dancing over rocks. And then I saw the bridge.

The same bridge, I realized a moment later, where Blue and I had found Mountain Dave. I recognized the delicate arch, the graceful railing. A bridge as elegant as any piece of garden sculpture ever built.

I blinked my eyes. Surely I was seeing things. There seemed to be light under the bridge. A soft, yellow glow. Not the white light of the moon, the warm light of fire.

But there couldn't be a fire under the bridge. Unless . . .

The two horses tugged forward toward the water. They were thirsty. I let them wade in and drink, staring in the direction of the bridge.

Sure enough, after a minute, I saw a figure emerge. A slender figure with long hair in a ponytail and an equally long beard.

"Mountain Dave?" I called tentatively.

"Who wants to know?" It was Dave's voice.

"It's Gail. I met you the other day. I was with Blue Winter, the tall, redheaded guy who used to ride bikes. We were tracking some horses; you called to let us know where they went." My voice trailed feebly on and on; Mountain Dave stood silent in the moonlight, a modern embodiment of Pan. I could almost see the hooves.

"I remember you," he said at last.

"I need help. The woman I told you we were tracking, she chased me in here and tried to shoot me. She's lying in a ravine at least five miles back that way." I waved a hand in the direction of the ridgeline. "And I'm exhausted. I don't think I can ride any farther." I heard the catch in my voice as I spoke the words; pressing my lips firmly together, I resisted the sobs I could feel rising.

Dave was silent for a moment.

Let him help me, I implored wordlessly, realizing how bizarre my story must sound. *Please.*

Perhaps bizarre wasn't a problem for Dave. As if he'd heard the plea, he answered, "I'll help you. Climb down off that horse and come on under the bridge. I've got a blanket there. You look cold."

"I am cold," I said. I slid off Leo and tied him and Paint to nearby trees.

"Can you ride your bike to get help?" I asked Dave tentatively.

"I can do better." I saw his teeth flash white in the moonlight. Reaching in the pocket of his pants, he produced an object that gleamed.

I jumped, caught by memories of Barbara and her gun, before I realized what I was seeing. The mysterious object was a cell phone.

"Will it work from here?" I asked.

"Not from this spot. But it will from the top of the ridge. And it will only take me five minutes to get there. I'll call the rangers and have them come get you."

"How will they know where to come?"

"Oh, everybody knows the Buddha Bridge."

"The Buddha Bridge?"

"Sure. Go look. And get the blanket."

After a minute, I walked obediently towards the bridge and ducked under its sheltering span.

I blinked. Several small votive candles illuminated the space with their flickering yellow light. They were arranged in a semicircle in front of a seated Buddha figure, who rested with his back to one end of the bridge. Someone—I suspected Mountain Dave—had placed a tiny bouquet of wild iris just where the Buddha could rest his eyes upon it.

Beyond the candles, in a flat, sandy spot, I could see an extremely lightweight sleeping bag. Footsteps alerted me to Dave's presence.

"I see why it's called the Buddha Bridge," I said. "Who put the statue there?"

"No one knows. It's been here as long as I've been roaming the park, and that's ten years now."

171

I stared at the figure. Just a foot-high concrete Buddha, faded and worn, the ordinary sort one could buy at garden centers, the statue had a delicate shawl of lichen and the soft patina of age and weather. Candlelight made the slight smile on his face seem to change from moment to moment. His eyes appeared to look right at me—and to look right through me.

Dave picked up the sleeping bag, unzipped it, and handed it to me. "It's clean," he said.

It did, indeed, look freshly laundered. I wrapped it gratefully around my shoulders. "Thanks," I said.

"I'll go make the call. You rest here."

"Okay. Be sure and tell them to send some kind of rescue crew for the woman; if she's alive, she's probably injured. And they should get hold of a Detective Matt Johnson with the sheriff's department. He'll want to be here. And we'll need a trailer for the horses. Oh, and please, can you call my boyfriend? He'll be worried sick."

Dave fished in his pocket and brought out the small notebook and stub of a pencil. "I've still got your phone number," he said. "What's the cop's name again?"

I told him. I gave him Blue's cell phone number, too.

"All right," he said. "I'll make the calls, then I'll come back and collect my stuff. When the troops get here, don't mention me, okay?"

"It's a promise. And thank you."

Mountain Dave picked up his bicycle, which lay in the sand next to the rudimentary camp he'd made under the bridge. In another moment he was on it and ascending the stream bank in the moonlight.

I watched in awe. Like one creature, man and bike scrambled up the steep trail. It was unearthly; again I thought of Pan. Pan, who is the protective god of all hooved and horned beings. I remembered the buck who had appeared to me on the trail. Pipe music seemed to tremble in the air.

Tired beyond my own understanding, I suddenly saw Mountain

Dave, the cycle tramp, as a shape-shifting shaman, entrusted with the secret of the lost bond between man and Nature, sent to save me in this hour of my deepest need. I took a deep breath. Who knows, I told myself. Truth and magic are intertwined. You don't need to figure this out. Just be grateful.

Wrapping the sleeping bag more closely around myself, I sat down in front of the Buddha to wait.

TWENTY-SEVEN

My rescue, when it came, was relatively uneventful. Dave and his camp vanished, just as he'd said he would, when ranger Jeeps growled up the old logging road in a blaze of headlights. Detective Johnson was with them and so, to my amazement, was Blue.

Hurrying to his side, I asked, "How'd you manage to get in here?"

"The detective and I were camped out in Paula King's living room when we got your message. We came together," Blue wrapped his arms around me. "Are you okay?"

"Yeah. I am. I'm sore as hell, but I'm fine."

Turning to Detective Johnson, who was at my elbow, I said, "I'll tell you the story as we go, but we need to look for Barbara King. If she's alive, she's probably injured."

In another minute I'd directed the rangers who had brought a horse trailer to take Paint and Leo back to Sandy's. Blue, Detective Johnson, and I climbed into another Jeep.

The ranger behind the wheel glanced at me briefly. "Dave gone?" he asked.

"Who?" I responded.

"Right." He started the Jeep and headed up the road.

I told my story as we jolted and bounced our way back over the country I'd just traversed on horseback. I left out only two details: Carlos Castillo and the fact that I'd purposefully spooked Barbara's horse. All else I recounted just as it happened, right up until the point I encountered Mountain Dave.

"How did you manage to call us?" Detective Johnson asked.

"I ran into a cyclist with a cell phone," I said.

The ranger snorted.

"What time is it, anyway?" I asked the group in general.

"It's two A.M.," the ranger replied.

"I got your call just after midnight," Blue added.

"You must have been worried." I squeezed his hand.

"I was," he said quietly.

"It's just over this ridge, I think," I told the driver.

It was surprisingly hard to pinpoint the spot where Barbara went over. Everything looked different, approaching from the opposite direction, safely ensconced in the Jeep. I found it hard to believe that only a few hours ago, I had been struggling to stay alive, here on this very hill.

In the end, I got out of the Jeep and backtracked on foot, finally spotting the big rock that I'd used as a shelter.

"Here," I said, pointing to the bank. "Her horse spooked right here. She fell off and went over the edge."

We all peered down. Moonlight poured over the lacy, patterned depths of the canyon; I could hear water on stone.

"Barbara!" I shouted.

No answer. Only the quiet voices of the night.

"We've got a rescue crew coming," Detective Johnson said at last. "They'll rappel down and have a look. Are you sure this is the place?"

"I'm sure," I said. "Real sure."

EPILOGUE

Barbara King didn't make it. The rescue crew found her body; appearances indicated she'd died in the fall. I never told anyone but Blue that I'd spooked her horse and caused her death, but I haven't forgotten. And I still believe that I did what I had to do.

Blue and I got married in June, in my garden. My cousin came out from Michigan; Blue's parents stood by our side. Roey and Freckles wore bows on their collars, and a good time was had by all at the party afterward.

For our honeymoon, we took the horses back to the old barn on Elkhorn Slough. Blue made margaritas, of course, and we touched our glasses together as the full moon rose over the water.

"Here's to you, Stormy," Blue said.

I took his hand. "Here's to us."